Thera's Final Days: A Story of Ash and Tides

Sarah Princeps

Published by Sarah Princeps, 2025.

THERA'S FINAL DAYS: A STORY OF ASH AND TIDES

First edition. March 3, 2025.

ISBN: 979-8230515845

Written by Sarah Princeps.

"The gods whisper in the trembling earth and the shifting sea, but love speaks in the quiet spaces between. When the heavens rage and the world burns, will you listen to fate—or to your own heart?"

Chapter 1: The High Priestess of Potnia

Callista Antheia stood before the sacred fire, her slender hands moving through the air with practiced grace as she performed the ancient ritual. The flickering flames danced across her face, casting shadows that accentuated her high cheekbones and the determined set of her jaw. Her emerald eyes reflected the fire's glow as she focused intently on interpreting the divine messages hidden within.

Around her, a circle of young acolytes watched in reverent silence, their gazes fixed upon their high priestess. Clad in simple white robes, the girls stood motionless, barely daring to breathe lest they disturb Callista's sacred communion with Potnia.

The temple filled with rhythmic chanting, with the acolytes' voices rising and falling in perfect unison. The ancient words flowed like a gentle stream, merging with the crackle of the flames and the soft rustle of Callista's robes. The harmonious sounds wove together, creating a mystical tapestry that enveloped the sanctuary.

Callista's mind drifted, attuning itself to the currents of divine wisdom that flowed from the fire. Images flashed behind her eyes—a glimpse of the future, a warning, a promise. She carefully sifted through each impression, her brow furrowing slightly as she sought to unravel their enigmatic meanings.

"The flames whisper of change," Callista murmured, her voice soft yet commanding. "Potnia speaks to us, my daughters. We must heed her call."

The acolytes exchanged glances, their eyes wide with a mix of excitement and apprehension. It was a great honor to be chosen as an acolyte of the high priestess, and they were eager to prove themselves worthy of the task.

As the chanting reached a crescendo, Callista raised her arms, her voice rising above the chorus. "Great Mother, guide us in your wisdom. Show us the path we must walk."

The flames leaped higher as if responding to her plea. Callista closed her eyes, allowing the heat to wash over her face. At that moment, she felt the presence of the goddess, a comforting warmth that filled her heart and soothed her mind.

As the ritual concluded, Callista lowered her arms, her heart filled with a profound sense of duty and devotion. She bowed her head, offering a silent prayer to Potnia, the Great Mother who guided their lives. The acolytes followed her lead, their heads dipping in unison as they joined in the reverent gesture. Callista's lips moved silently, her prayer a private conversation between herself and the goddess. She sought strength, wisdom, and clarity to navigate the challenges ahead. The weight of her responsibilities settled on her shoulders, but it was a burden she bore with grace and determination.

With a final whispered word, Callista lifted her head and turned to face the altar. She reached out, her fingertips grazing the ancient stone, feeling the energy that pulsed within it. It was a reminder of the sacred bond between the priestesses and the divine, a connection that had endured for generations.

Stepping away from the altar, Callista's movements were fluid and purposeful. Her long robes swayed with each step, the fabric whispering against the polished floor. She approached a group of villagers who waited nearby, their faces etched with a mix of hope and uncertainty.

"High Priestess," a woman said, bowing her head respectfully. "We seek your guidance."

Callista smiled warmly, her eyes softening with compassion. "Speak, my child. I am here to listen."

The woman wrung her hands, her gaze darting nervously. "The crops, High Priestess. They wither in the fields, and the rains have not come. We fear for our sustenance."

Callista nodded, her expression thoughtful. She reached out, placing a gentle hand on the woman's shoulder. "The cycles of nature are not always kind, but we must have faith. Potnia sees our struggles and hears our prayers."

Her words were met with murmurs of agreement from the gathered villagers. They drew comfort from her presence, finding solace in her calm assurance.

"I will offer prayers for the rains to come," Callista said, her voice carrying a note of determination. "In the meantime, let us work together to conserve what we have and support one another. The strength of our community lies in our unity."

The villagers nodded, their faces brightening with renewed hope. Callista moved among them, listening to their concerns and offering words of encouragement. She knew that her role extended beyond the temple walls into the lives of those she served.

Callista's mind turned to the challenges ahead as she listened to their troubles. The strange tremors beneath the temple, the whispers of change in the flames—these were omens that could not be ignored. She knew that her path as high priestess would be filled with trials and difficult decisions. But in that moment, surrounded by the faces of her people, Callista found strength in their trust and faith. She silently vowed to be the leader they needed, to guide them through whatever storms may come. With Potnia's blessing and the support of her community, she would face the future with unwavering resolve.

A soft voice drew Callista's attention. "High Priestess, may I speak with you?" A young woman stepped forward, her eyes cast downward in deference.

Callista smiled warmly, placing a gentle hand on the woman's shoulder. "Of course, my child. What troubles you?"

The woman, Melina, raised her gaze, revealing eyes brimming with unshed tears. "It's my husband, Priestess. He... he hasn't returned from his fishing voyage. It's been days, and I fear the worst."

Callista's heart ached for Melina. She knew the pain of uncertainty all too well. "Let us walk together," she said, guiding Melina to a quiet corner of the temple courtyard.

As they stood beneath the dappled shade of an olive tree, Callista listened intently as Melina poured out her fears and worries. The young woman's hands trembled as she spoke of their two small children, of the hardships they would face without her husband's support.

Callista took Melina's hands in her own, her touch radiating comfort and understanding. "I cannot promise his safe return," she said softly, "but I can offer you the strength to endure, no matter what the future holds."

Melina's tears flowed freely now, but her eyes showed a glimmer of hope. "Thank you, Priestess. Your words bring me solace in this dark time."

Callista embraced the young woman, offering a silent prayer to Potnia for her well-being. As Melina took her leave, Callista's thoughts turned inward. How many more families would face such trials in the days to come?

A familiar figure caught Callista's eye, drawing her from her contemplation. Priestess Eirene approached, her silver hair gleaming in the sunlight. There was a serenity to her movements, a grace born of decades in Potnia's service.

Yet as Eirene approached, Callista sensed an undercurrent of tension in her former mentor's bearing. The older priestess's brow furrowed, her lips pressed into a thin line. Something weighed heavily on her mind.

"Callista," Eirene said, her voice low and urgent. "We must speak in private. There are matters of great import that cannot wait."

Callista nodded, a sense of unease settling in her stomach. She knew that look in Eirene's eyes all too well. It was the look of someone who had gazed into the heart of the flames and seen the shadows of things to come.

Together, the two priestesses made their way towards the temple's inner sanctum, their footsteps echoing against the ancient stones. Whatever news Eirene brought, Callista knew that it would test the very foundations of her faith and leadership.

But she was ready to face the challenge head-on, armed with the strength of her convictions and the unwavering support of her people. Come what may, she would lead them through the storm.

As the heavy wooden doors of the inner sanctum closed behind them, Callista turned to face Eirene. The older priestess's face was etched with concern, her blue eyes troubled.

"What is it, Eirene?" Callista asked, her voice steady despite the rising sense of apprehension in her chest. "What have you seen?"

Eirene sighed, her shoulders sagging as if under a great weight. "The tremors, Callista. They grow more frequent with each passing day. The very foundations of the temple shudder beneath our feet."

Callista frowned, her mind racing. She had felt the tremors, too, a subtle vibration that seemed to emanate from the very heart of the island. At first, she had dismissed them as a mere curiosity, a quirk of the ancient stones. But now, with Eirene's words, a sense of foreboding settled over her like a shroud.

"What do you believe they portend?" Callista asked, her voice barely above a whisper.

Eirene shook her head, her silver hair catching the light of the flickering candles. "I cannot say for certain. But I fear that they are an omen of great change, of upheaval to come."

Callista's mind whirled with the implications of Eirene's words. As the high priestess, it was her duty to interpret the signs and guide her people through whatever challenges lay ahead. But the tremors were unlike anything she had encountered before, a mystery that seemed to defy the very laws of nature. She closed her eyes, seeking the calming presence of Potnia in her heart. But even as she reached out to the goddess, she could feel the weight of her responsibilities pressing down upon her, the burden of leadership that she had borne since the day she had first donned the sacred robes.

"What would you have me do, Eirene?" Callista asked, her voice barely above a whisper. "How can I lead our people through this uncertainty?"

Eirene placed a warm and reassuring hand on Callista's shoulder. "You must trust in yourself, Callista, in the wisdom that Potnia has bestowed upon you. The answers will come in time."

Callista nodded, drawing strength from her mentor's words. She knew that the path ahead would be difficult, that the tremors were but the first sign of the challenges to come. But with Potnia's guidance and the support of her people, she would face whatever lay ahead with courage and resolve. A heavy silence descended upon the room, broken only by the soft crackling of the sacred fire. The air grew thick with the mingled scents of incense and uncertainty as if the very temple itself held its breath in anticipation.

Callista's gaze drifted to the intricate frescoes adorning the walls. Their vibrant colors suddenly became muted in the face of the looming unknown. The figures seemed to dance and shift in the flickering light, their movements echoing the restless energy coursing through her veins.

Beside her, Eirene stood motionless, her silver hair gleaming like a beacon of wisdom in the dimly lit chamber. Her usually calm and serene eyes now held a glimmer of concern, reflecting the unspoken fears that hung between them. "The tremors are but a whisper of what is to come," Eirene murmured, her voice barely audible above the soft rustling of her robes. "The gods are speaking to us, Callista. We must listen."

Callista nodded, her mind racing with the implications of Eirene's words. She had always trusted in the guidance of the gods, in the sacred bond that connected her to the divine. But now, faced with an omen so powerful and mysterious, she felt a flicker of doubt, a tiny crack in the foundation of her faith.

"And if we cannot understand their message?" Callista asked, her voice trembling slightly. "What then?"

Eirene's eyes met hers, a knowing smile playing at the corners of her lips. "Then we must have faith, my child. Faith in ourselves, in each other, and in the wisdom of the gods."

The words hung in the air between them, a lifeline of hope amid the gathering darkness. Callista drew a deep breath, letting the familiar scent of incense fill her lungs and calm her racing thoughts.

"You are right, of course," she said, her voice growing stronger with each word. "We must not let fear cloud our judgment. We must be the light that guides our people through this time of uncertainty."

Eirene nodded, pride shining in her eyes. "And you, Callista, will be that light. Trust in yourself, and in the path that Potnia has laid before you."

As the two women stood together, their silhouettes illuminated by the dancing flames, Callista felt a renewed sense of purpose flowing through her. The tremors may have shaken the very foundations of their world, but she would not let them shake her resolve. With Eirene's wisdom and the strength of her own faith, she would lead her people through whatever trials lay ahead, guided by the eternal light of the gods.

Callista bowed her head, her voice filled with genuine appreciation. "Thank you, Eirene. Your counsel means more to me than I can express. I will seek further guidance from the goddess and do all in my power to protect our people."

Eirene placed a gentle hand on Callista's shoulder, a gesture of support and understanding. "I have every confidence in you, High Priestess. Remember, you are not alone in this. The strength of our community lies in our unity."

With a final nod, Eirene turned and departed, her silver hair glinting in the flickering light of the braziers as she passed through the temple doors. Callista watched her go, feeling a mixture of gratitude and trepidation.

As the sound of Eirene's footsteps faded, Callista turned her gaze back to the sacred fire. The flames danced and twisted, casting shifting shadows across the intricate frescoes that adorned the temple walls. She stared into the heart of the fire, seeking the guidance and wisdom she so desperately needed.

Questions swirled through her mind, each one more pressing than the last. What did the tremors portend? Were they a sign of Potnia's displeasure or a warning of some more significant danger to come? As High Priestess, it fell to her to interpret the signs and guide her people through whatever challenges lay ahead.

The weight of her responsibilities settled heavily upon her shoulders, a mantle she had worn with pride since the day she had been chosen to lead the cult of Potnia. But never before had she felt the burden so keenly. As if in response to her thoughts, another tremor rumbled through the temple, causing the flames to flicker and dance. Callista closed her eyes, reaching out with her senses to the very heart of the sacred isle.

And there, beneath the surface, she felt it. A pulse of ancient power, a whisper of something stirring in the depths. The tremors were a herald of its awakening, a sign that the world was on the brink of change. Callista's eyes snapped open, her heart racing with a mixture of fear and determination. Whatever was coming, she would face it head-on. For the sake of her people, for the sake of all she held dear, she would be the light in the darkness.

Chapter 2: Stranger from the Sea

The harbor of Akrotiri was a bustling hub of activity, with ships of various sizes and shapes docked at its piers. Though small compared to many of Thera's other ports, the village and harbor of Akrotiri were still of great significance to the island's economy. Waves crashed against the walls, creating a mesmerizing display of white foam against the dark stone. In the distance, the lighthouse stands tall and proud, guiding ships through the stormy sea. The water was a deep blue, reflecting the cloudy grey sky above. Tiny houses and buildings lined the edges of the harbor, buzzing with movement and energy.

The salty brine of the sea mingled with the musty smell of the wooden piers. The scent of freshly caught fish wafts through the air, mixing with the warm aroma of bread baking in nearby ovens. The smell of salt and seaweed fills the air, a familiar and comforting scent to those who call the small harbor town home. It was a sanctuary of sorts, a place where sailors and merchants could rest and find shelter from the tempestuous sea and where the salty tang of the ocean mingled with the sweet scent of olives on the gentle breeze.

But today was different. Captain Minoas Lysandros stood like a steadfast beacon at the edge of Akrotiri's Harbor. His gaze piercing through the veil of rain that the heavens had unceremoniously unleashed upon them. The sea churned with a ferocity only Poseidon himself could muster, and the wind played a furious symphony that seemed to shake the very soul of the island. Yet there, amidst the tempest's tantrum, a ship danced dangerously with the waves, its sails tattered like the wings of an injured seagull.

"By Potnia's grace, not on my watch," Minoas murmured under his breath, his voice almost snatched away by the howling gales.

"Men! To stations! To the boats!" His command cut through the cacophony with the precision of a well-thrown spear. "There are lives calling out for our hands!"

Given the speed with which his crew sprang into action, he might as well have been calling them to a feast. Ropes were gathered with the deftness of seasoned weavers, and small rescue boats were readied as if they themselves shared in the urgency of their masters' hearts.

"Keep your wits as sharp as your filet knives, boys!" he called out, a twinkle of humor lighting up his eyes despite the grim situation. "The sea's serving up a mighty stew today, and we're to pluck the olives from it!"

The men chuckled amidst their haste, for even nature's wrath couldn't dampen the warmth that Captain Minoas exuded. He was a pillar of strength wrapped in the comfort of a familiar blanket. With ropes coiled over shoulders and oars in hand, his crew followed him, their movements synchronized with the ease of a dance they'd performed a hundred times under less dire circumstances.

"Steady now, let's show these waves the mettle of Thera's sons!" Minoas directed, his voice a steady drumbeat over the storm's roar.

As the first boat pushed off into the frothing waters, each man paddled with the fervor of one fighting for more than just the lives of strangers. They rowed to the rhythm of survival, the beat of hope against despair, led by a captain whose heart was as vast as the sea itself.

***

The deck beneath Dorian Xenophon pitched wildly like a living creature trying to shake off its unwelcome guests. His vessel, the Althea, once a proud merchant ship that had danced upon gentler waves, now seemed a plaything of the gods' fury. The timbers, which had faithfully borne countless cargoes across the Mediterranean's embrace, groaned in protest as the storm hammered them with relentless force.

"Brace yourselves!" Dorian's voice was a clarion call amidst the cacophony of wind and water. His crew, a band of men as diverse as the ports they'd hailed from, rallied around his unyielding determination.

His hands, weathered by rope and brine, held the wheel with a lover's grasp as if willing the wood to find a strength it no longer possessed.

"Land must be near! Eyes sharp!" he shouted over the tempest's howl, even as the salt spray stung his eyes like the thousand pinpricks of an unforgiving sea.

But the Althea, much like the mythic heroes of old, was not destined for a quiet end. A monstrous wave rose before them, a watery colossus with the might of Poseidon's trident behind it. It towered with a roar that drowned out all else, a liquid mountain against which human efforts seemed pitifully small.

"By the gods..." a crewman murmured, his words snatched away by the wind.

"Steady!" Dorian commanded, locking his gaze on the approaching doom. "We ride this one out together!"

As the wave crashed down, the world turned to chaos. The impact was thunderous. Wood splintered with the violence of thunderclaps, the ship's proud mast snapping like the bone of a fallen warrior. The Althea, mortally wounded, veered toward the cliffs that loomed like jagged teeth waiting to feed.

"Abandon—" Dorian's command was cut short as the sea claimed him, swallowing his form into its frothing maw. The crew, those seasoned sons of the tide, were cast adrift in the angry waters, flailing for purchase where none could be found.

In the heart of the turmoil, Dorian fought. He battled not just for breath but for every story untold, every port unvisited, every hand unshaken. His charismatic smile was hidden by the grim set of his jaw, a warrior's resolve etched onto his features as he sought the surface, reaching for life amid the indifferent waves.

Yet, above, the storm raged on, indifferent to the mortals' plight, a symphony of nature's raw power playing out upon the stage of the Aegean Sea.

***

High Priestess Callista's ceremonial robes fluttered in the storm's fury. Her eyes were wide as she saw the tragedy unfolding off Akrotiri's rugged coast. The ceremony she had been leading—a plea to Potnia for bountiful harvests—was now a distant echo, replaced by the immediate need to save lives.

"Come!" she urged her acolytes, her voice carrying over the howl of the winds. "The sea shows no mercy, but we must offer ours."

Her acolytes, young women robed in the white of Potnia's service, hesitated only a moment before rallying behind their High Priestess. Together, they hastened down to the harbor, where the waves crashed against the shore like furious titans at war.

As they approached the chaos, Callista's gaze found Captain Minoas Lysandros, his form a steadfast presence against the tempest. His movements were fluid and decisive, betraying none of the fear that surely clenched at every heart watching the ordeal.

"Captain," Callista called out, her tone even as if she were still within the sacred confines of the temple rather than amidst nature's wrath. "How may we aid you?"

"High Priestess," he responded, sparing her a nod that conveyed both respect and urgency. "We need strong hands and willing hearts. Ropes, blankets, and steadiness amidst the panic."

"Then you shall have them," she affirmed.

Callista turned to her followers, her words slicing through the cacophony with serene authority. "Gather ropes and linens from the storerooms. Bring them to the water's edge with haste!"

As the acolytes scattered to follow her command, Callista stepped closer to Minoas, her eyes tracking the violent ebb and flow of the waters. She lifted her arms skyward, her voice rising in prayer.

"Great Mother, who commands the earth, the sea, and the sky, lend us your strength. Protect these souls in their hour of need."

Minoas watched her briefly, respect etched across his seasoned features, before returning his attention to the task at hand. The storm might be deaf to mortal pleas, but the High Priestess's unshakable faith offered comfort.

"Your voice brings calm, High Priestess," he said gruffly, his eyes never leaving the tumultuous sea. "But we'll need more than prayers to pull them from Poseidon's grasp."

"Prayers are but the beginning," Callista replied, her green eyes reflecting the steel of her resolve. "Now let us tend to their earthly forms."

With the acolytes returning, laden with supplies, Callista's composure remained a beacon of hope as she directed their efforts, her presence the embodiment of Potnia's grace amidst the storm's relentless rage.

Callista and the other priestesses who were to help her in the water shed their robes, and strode into the water. Cold and insistent, the water surged around her, but it did not deter her. She moved with purpose, her eyes fixed on the figure bobbing helplessly in the churning waves ahead.

"Keep your head above water!" she called out, her voice surprisingly steady over the roar of the storm. As the high priestess of Potnia, she was no stranger to command, even if her usual domain was the temple rather than the treacherous sea.

Dorian fought against the tide's pull, flailing his arms to stay afloat. He caught sight of Callista, her dark hair plastered to her face by the rain, her green eyes fierce with determination. This naked woman seemed to be a visage pulled straight from myths and the stories told by old men haggard by the sea. Yet, even as he struggled, there was something magnetic about her presence, a spark of recognition that flickered to life between them amidst the tempest's fury.

"Almost there!" she encouraged, reaching out as a wave lifted him closer. Their hands met, fingers interlocking, and for a moment, the chaos around them seemed to still. It was as if the very heart of the storm recognized the connection being forged in its midst.

With Callista's guidance, Dorian managed to find his footing, though the sea seemed reluctant to release him from its grasp. Together, they turned back toward the shore, where Minoas and the other rescuers had formed multiple human chains with the ropes to retrieve survivors.

"Lean on me," Callista said, her arm supportive around Dorian's waist as they staggered through the water. Her acolytes, worked alongside fishermen and townswomen, their efforts synchronized by a shared purpose.

"Thank you," Dorian gasped, his breaths coming in short bursts. "I owe you my life."

"Let's secure it first," she replied, a hint of warmth in her tone despite the grim circumstances.

They reached the safety of the shore, where strong hands pulled them onto firmer ground. Dorian collapsed beside other shivering figures who had been plucked from the sea's icy clutches. Callista knelt beside him, her robe heavy and sodden, yet her spirit undimmed.

"Rest now," she said softly, brushing wet strands of hair from his forehead. "You are under Potnia's protection."

As the cold clothes were stripped off the survivors and taken to be dried, blankets were draped over them, and hot tea and mulled wines were pressed into trembling hands. Callista stood watch, her gaze sweeping over each rescued soul. The storm railed on, still hungry for havoc, but within the circle of Therans, there was a tangible sense of relief.

"High Priestess," Minoas said, joining her side, "your bravery is matched only by your faith."

"Today, we are all servants of Potnia," Callista responded, her eyes reflecting the fading lightning. "But perhaps tomorrow, we can find some humor in a high priestess playing the part of a fisherman."

Minoas chuckled, the sound mingling with the wind. "I'll hold you to that."

The storm began to relent, its once furious howling now just weary sighs against the cliffs. As calm settled over Akrotiri, Callista allowed herself a small, victorious smile as she, the fisherman, sailors, her priestesses, and other townspeople dried themselves and put their discarded clothing back on. Today had brought destruction, but in its wake, the seeds of new beginnings were already taking root.

As the survivors huddled together, their breaths misting in the cool air, a figure detached himself from the shadows cast by the flickering torches lining the harbor. Lykos Theodoros's steely gaze swept over the scene before him, his aquiline nose lifted ever so slightly as if to scent the wind of change that the storm had brought to Akrotiri. His gray eyes, sharp and unyielding, fixed on the newcomers with an intensity that belied his composed exterior.

"Quite the tempest, isn't it?" he remarked, approaching Minoas and Callista with a stride that mirrored the confidence of his station. His robes, richly adorned yet untouched by the chaos, whispered against the damp cobblestones.

"Indeed," Minoas replied, shocked at the sudden appearance of the Priest-King of Thera himself. "But even the fiercest storm bows before Thera's resolve."

"Spoken like a true son of the sea," Lykos said, allowing a thin smile to touch his lips. And you, High Priestess," he turned to Callista. "Your courage today honors Potnia. Yet I must ask..." He paused, looking out at the wreckage bobbing in the water. "From whence did these unfortunate souls emerge?"

"From beyond our sight, guided here by fate or fortune," Callista responded her voice a soothing balm amidst the lingering disquiet of the storm. "We were but instruments of Potnia's will, aiding those in need."

"Ah, yes." Lykos nodded, his eyes narrowing slightly. "Fate or fortune — intriguing possibilities, indeed. And do we know who they are? Their purpose on our sacred isle?"

"Determined spirits, seeking refuge from Poseidon's wrath, or simply men on their way here or places further on for trade." Minoas interjected, his tone neutral yet firm. "Their vessel was no match for such fury."

"Of course." Lykos's reply was smooth as polished marble, but there was a hardness there, too. "It would be wise to learn more, don't you think? A shipwreck is no small matter, especially when it brings strangers to our shores, now stranded here. No longer mere merchant visitors."

"Every soul has a story," Callista said, meeting Lykos's gaze with unwavering tranquility. "In time, we shall hear theirs. For now, let us be grateful for their lives spared."

"Gratitude and caution make fine bedfellows," Lykos conceded, the hint of a warning threaded through his words. "I trust you both will ensure these... guests... respect the ways of Thera."

"Rest assured, we shall extend every hospitality—and wisdom," Minoas assured him, clapping a hand on Callista's shoulder with companionable ease that contrasted with the tension between the three.

"Excellent." Lykos stepped back, reclaiming his personal space with the precision of a temple ritual. "Then I leave this matter in your capable hands. May Potnia guide us all."

As he retreated into the night, the last vestiges of the storm seemed to follow, leaving behind a newfound stillness that wrapped around the island like a protective shawl. Minoas and Callista exchanged a brief look—a silent acknowledgment of the delicate dance ahead.

Callista moved through the survivors and found the young man she had pulled from the sea. Warmth spread through Callista's fingers as she clasped Dorian's hands, helping him to a sitting position on the coarse sand of Akrotiri's harbor. The storm had receded enough to allow a faint gleam of moonlight to dance across his drenched features, casting a silver glow on his grateful smile.

"By the gods, I owe you my life," Dorian spoke, his voice roughened by saltwater and wind yet imbued with an unmistakable warmth. "Both of you." He turned his gaze toward Minoas, who stood nearby, his stance relaxed despite the evening's harrowing events.

"Think nothing of it," Minoas replied with a dismissive wave—a captain to his core, unshaken even by Poseidon's tempestuous mood swings. "The sea gives, and the sea takes. Today, it saw fit to spare you."

"Yet, it was not the sea but your bravery and the grace of the priestess that delivered us from its depths," Dorian insisted. His hand gestured toward the dark expanse of water behind them, still roiling with the storm's last whispers. "I am in your debt. Please, tell me how I might repay such kindness."

"Your safety is enough of a reward," Callista said, though her heart fluttered like a dove caught in sudden updrafts at his earnest eyes. She couldn't help but notice the way they seemed to capture the very essence of the horizon—vast, mysterious, and beckoning.

"Time is a generous gift," Dorian said, a spark igniting in his eyes that matched the stars above. "Thank you for giving it to me. My name is Dorian."

Callista felt her breath catch, the air between them charged with something ancient yet unfamiliar. A sensation she'd read about in countless scrolls but had never truly understood until now. She drew back ever so slightly, reminding herself that some boundaries were not meant to be crossed—not easily, anyway. "I am Callista, High Priestess of the Temple of Potnia in the Capital." Dorian's eyes widened at the knowledge of her high station.

"Rest now," she offered, her words carrying the gentle firmness that had comforted many before him. "Tomorrow, the sun will rise on your new beginning here."

"Indeed," Dorian agreed, his smile lingering as he allowed the priestesses to guide him toward shelter and warmth.

As she watched him go, lithe and resilient despite the ordeal, Callista felt the weight of her ceremonial robes like never before, heavy with responsibility and expectation. Yet beneath it all, there was an undeniable thread of excitement weaving through her thoughts—a curiosity awakened by this stranger who had been tossed upon their shores by fate's own hand.

The fury of the storm had dwindled to a murmur. Captain Minoas Lysandros stood once more at the edge of Akrotiri's harbor, his gaze following the receding clouds as they released their final, feeble grumbles. A soft light peeked through the dispersing gray, painting the sky with strokes of orange and pink—a canvas promising renewal.

"Seems Potnia herself has been appeased," he mused aloud, a half-smile playing on his lips as he turned to see the survivors huddled in blankets, shivering but alive.

"Or perhaps she's merely catching her breath," Callista replied from beside him, her eyes reflecting the palette of dawn. "For now, we must tend to those she's spared."

The islanders moved about with quiet efficiency, offering bread and fish, stoking fires, and sharing the warmth of woven cloaks. The rhythm of life in Akrotiri resumed its steady tempo like a familiar tune hummed under one's breath.

Now wrapped in a coarse blanket that did little to hide the robust frame beneath, Dorian Xenophon watched this dance of generosity with appreciative eyes. His voice carried over, clear and tinged with that indefinable quality that drew people to him. "Your home has weathered many storms, I presume?" he asked a fisherman who was checking his nets for damage.

"Ah, the sea gives us tales to tell our grandkids," the fisherman chuckled, knotting a frayed section with deft fingers. "And sometimes, it sends us mysteries wrapped in waves."

"I agree, my home does much the same for our people!" Dorian agreed, his smile not dimming despite the ache in his bones. He looked out over the water as if seeing beyond the horizon, where his own stories lay waiting to be retold.

From a short distance away, Lykos Theodoros watched the exchange, his expression unreadable. His eyes, sharp as a hawk's, seemed to pierce through the mist of conviviality that enshrouded the newcomers. With every word exchanged, every laugh shared, the lines on his forehead deepened ever so slightly.

"Curious sort, aren't they?" Minoas said, approaching Lykos with an ease that belied the tension between them.

"Curiosity can be as perilous as any storm, Captain," Lykos replied smoothly, his gaze still locked on Dorian. "Understanding what winds have pushed these travelers to our shore would serve us well."

"Understanding is the anchor of wisdom, or so the scrolls say," Callista chimed in, joining the two men. Her voice was serene, yet beneath it flowed currents of caution.

"But let us not forget that some anchors can also drag us down into the depths." Lykos echoed, his tone mirroring the cool touch of the breeze. With a last, lingering look, he turned on his heel, his robes whispering secrets only they could hear.

As the first rays of sunlight stretched across the land, kissing the white-washed walls of Akrotiri with warmth, a subtle shift hung in the air, like the change in the key of a well-known melody. Callista felt it, a tremor of anticipation—or was it trepidation?—that threaded through the fabric of the day.

"Change is never without its challenges," she said, primarily to herself, watching Lykos's retreating form.

"Let us hope the scales tip in our favor," Minoas said, casting a sailor's wary eye toward the horizon where the sea met the sky in an unspoken truce.

Chapter 3: Visions of Change

Soft footsteps echoed through the marbled halls as High Priestess Callista entered the inner sanctum. The flickering light from bronze oil lamps danced across the intricately carved walls, casting long shadows that seemed to come alive with the stories of the gods. Callista moved with graceful purpose, the weight of recent events and the enigmatic stranger heavy on her mind.

She settled onto an embroidered cushion, folding her legs beneath her as she had countless times before. The polished stone floor felt cool against her skin. Ornate braziers stood sentinel around her, their glowing embers releasing fragrant plumes of frankincense and myrrh. The heady scent filled her lungs with each breath, transporting her to a timeless place between realms.

"Great Potnia, Mother of Earth and Sea, hear your daughter's call," Callista intoned, her melodic voice seeming to resonate with the very walls of the sacred chamber. Verdant eyes drifted closed as she surrendered herself to the rituals of communion ingrained since childhood.

Yet even as the familiar words fell from her lips, Callista's thoughts strayed to the mysterious arrival who called himself Dorian. Something about his easy charm and knowing eyes both intrigued and unsettled her. Shaking her head slightly, she refocused on her invocations.

"Guide me in these uncertain times," she whispered. "Grant me the wisdom to interpret your signs and the strength to protect your people."

The flames swayed hypnotically as if dancing to an unheard rhythm. Callista's breathing slowed, each inhale drawing her deeper into a trance. She could feel the presence of the divine gathering around her like a cloak, ancient and powerful. The material world fell away until there was only the shimmering darkness behind her eyelids and the thrum of destiny in her veins.

In that liminal space between planes, Callista awaited the visions that would chart the course of her people's fate. And perhaps her own as well.

A sudden, searing burst of light flooded Callista's inner vision, the intensity nearly jolting her from her meditative state. Flames, ravenous and all-consuming, devoured the once-tranquil landscape of Thera. The sky seemed to bleed, an angry crimson hue pulsing with ominous energy.

The ground beneath her etheric feet trembled, and a deep, guttural growl resonated in her bones. Fissures snaked across the earth, widening into gaping maws that threatened to swallow everything in their path. The roar of the splitting land mingled with the terrified screams of the island's inhabitants, a cacophony of destruction and despair.

Callista's astral form moved through the chaos, an unseen witness to the unfolding catastrophe. Once proud and gleaming, the temples crumbled to dust before her eyes. The lush vineyards and olive groves withered and turned to ash, their fertile bounty reduced to mere memory.

In the heart of the devastation, a towering figure emerged, cloaked in shadows and wreathed in an aura of ancient power. Its presence seemed to draw the very life force from the land, leaving only desolation in its wake. Callista strained to make out the entity's details, but the vision shifted and blurred, denying her a clear view.

"Potnia, guide me," Callista's spirit cried out, her voice lost amidst the clamor of the apocalyptic scene. "What is the meaning of this? How can I prevent such a fate?"

The figure turned, its gaze piercing through the ethereal veil and locking onto Callista's. Molten and unfathomable eyes bore into her very essence, and a voice that was both everywhere and nowhere at once echoed through the dreamscape.

"The path ahead is shrouded in shadow, dear Callista," the voice intoned, each word a ripple in the fabric of the vision. "To save your people, you must first unravel the mysteries that lie within yourself and those who cross your path. Trust in the wisdom of the Mother, for She shall guide you through the trials to come."

The vision dissipated as suddenly as it had begun, leaving Callista gasping and shaken on the temple floor. The flickering oil lamps cast dancing shadows across her sweat-dampened brow, and the scent of incense hung heavy in the air, now tinged with an undercurrent of foreboding.

Callista's heart raced, pounding against her ribcage like a trapped bird desperate for escape. She drew in deep, shuddering breaths, her hands trembling as she pushed herself up from the cool marble floor. The lingering images of the vision danced before her eyes, the acrid scent of smoke and the thunder of crumbling stone still vivid in her mind.

She staggered to her feet, her legs unsteady beneath her. The once-comforting walls of the sanctum now felt confining, as if they might collapse inward at any moment. Callista's thoughts whirled, fragments of the divine message tumbling over one another in a dizzying cacophony.

"I must find Eirene," she whispered, her voice hoarse and strained. "She can help me decipher this vision."

With a newfound sense of purpose, Callista gathered her robes and strode from the chamber, her footsteps echoing through the hallowed halls. She navigated the winding corridors of the temple with practiced ease, her destination clear in her mind. The weight of the vision hung heavy upon her shoulders, a burden she knew she must share with her most trusted confidante.

As she approached Eirene's quarters, Callista paused, her hand poised to knock upon the weathered wooden door. A flicker of doubt crept into her heart, a momentary hesitation born of the knowledge that the vision would become all too real once spoken aloud. She drew a steadying breath, steeling herself for the conversation.

"Eirene?" Callista called out, her voice sounding small and distant to her own ears. "I must speak with you. It's urgent."

The soft rustle of fabric and the gentle padding of footsteps heralded Eirene's approach. The door swung open, revealing the elderly priestess, her silver hair gleaming in the soft light of the corridor. Eirene's eyes, deep pools of wisdom and compassion, met Callista's own, and at that moment, the high priestess felt a wave of relief wash over her.

"Callista, my dear," Eirene said, her voice a soothing balm to Callista's frayed nerves. "Come inside. Tell me what troubles you."

As Callista crossed the threshold into Eirene's chambers, she knew that no matter what challenges lay ahead, she would not face them alone. With the help of her old mentor and the strength of her convictions, she would unravel the mysteries of the vision and find a way to protect her beloved people from the impending doom that loomed on the horizon.

Callista stepped into Eirene's chambers, the familiar scent of sage and lavender enveloping her like a comforting embrace. The elder priestess gestured for Callista to sit beside her on the intricately woven cushions that adorned the stone bench beneath the window.

"I've had a vision, Eirene," Callista began, her voice trembling slightly. "One of great destruction and chaos. Flames consumed the sky, and the earth shook with a fury I've never known."

Eirene nodded, her expression pensive. "Tell me more, child. What did you see?"

"The ground split open, and I could hear the roar of the earth itself. It was as if the very foundations of our world were crumbling." Callista's hands trembled as she recounted the details, the images still vivid in her mind's eye.

Eirene reached out, placing a reassuring hand on Callista's arm. "Visions from the goddess can be powerful and unsettling. It's important to remember that they are not always literal, but rather a glimpse into the potential that lies ahead."

Callista met Eirene's gaze, her own eyes filled with a mix of awe and apprehension. "But what if it is a warning? A portent of things to come? I cannot stand idly by and watch as our people face such a fate."

"Nor should you," Eirene agreed, her voice calm and measured. "But we must approach this with wisdom and caution. Divine messages are often complex, layered with meanings that may not be immediately clear."

Callista sighed, her shoulders sagging under the weight of her newfound knowledge. "I fear for our people, Eirene. For our way of life. How can I lead them when I myself am so uncertain?"

Eirene smiled, a gentle curve of her lips that held both understanding and encouragement. "By trusting in the goddess and in yourself. You were chosen for this role, Callista, not only for your gifts but for your strength of spirit. The path ahead may be difficult, but you have the wisdom and compassion to guide our people through whatever trials may come."

As Callista listened to Eirene's words, a flicker of hope ignited within her heart. Perhaps the vision was not a certainty but a possibility, one that she could work to prevent. With the support of her mentor and the strength of her own convictions, she would face the challenges ahead, one step at a time.

***

The sun-drenched streets of Pyrgos Kallistis hummed with activity as Dorian wove his way through the bustling crowds. His eyes sparkled with curiosity, eager to absorb every detail of this vibrant city. While most of the crew that made it off Dorian's doomed ship had taken on with other ships and crews to work their way home, Dorian had accepted the invitation of the Captain and High Priestess to see the Capital and be their guest for a while. The air was filled with the mingled scents of spices and freshly baked bread and the chatter of locals haggling at market stalls.

"You there, young man!" A weathered voice called out from a nearby stall. "You look like someone who appreciates fine craftsmanship."

Dorian turned to see an elderly man gesturing towards an array of intricately woven baskets. He approached with a warm smile. "Indeed, I do. These are beautiful. Did you make them yourself?"

The old man chuckled, his eyes crinkling at the corners. "With these hands, I've been weaving baskets since before you were born. Each one tells a story, you know."

"I'd love to hear those stories," Dorian said, picking up a basket and admiring the delicate patterns. "I'm always eager to learn about local traditions."

As the old man regaled him with tales of the island's history, Dorian found himself captivated. He asked questions, listening intently to the answers and committing each detail to memory. The old man's face lit up, delighted to have found such an attentive audience.

Moving on, Dorian's ears caught the rhythmic chanting emanating from the temple. The sound was haunting and beautiful, drawing him closer. He paused at the entrance, marveling at the intricate carvings adorning the stone walls.

A young acolyte, her robes swirling around her ankles, noticed his interest. "The chants are an offering to Potnia," she explained, her voice filled with reverence. "They carry our prayers to her divine ears."

Dorian nodded, his expression one of genuine respect. "It's a powerful thing, to be so connected to one's faith. I admire the devotion of your people."

The acolyte smiled, pleased by his understanding. "Perhaps you'd like to learn more about our beliefs? I could show you around the temple, if you wish."

"I would be honored," Dorian replied, his heart swelling with gratitude for the opportunity to delve deeper into the Theran way of life.

As he followed the acolyte into the temple, Dorian couldn't help but feel a sense of belonging. The openness and warmth of the people he'd met so far made him feel welcome as if he were a part of something greater than himself. He knew, without a doubt, that his time on this island would be a journey of discovery, not just of the land, but of the spirit that made it so special.

From the shadowed recesses of the temple, Callista watched as Dorian entered, her keen eyes following his every move. She had been observing him from afar, intrigued by the way he seamlessly blended into the fabric of Theran life. His genuine interest in their customs and his respectful demeanor set him apart from the occasional foreign traders who passed through their shores.

As Dorian engaged in conversation with the young acolyte, Callista found herself drawn to the warmth of his smile and the ease with which he connected with others. It was a rare quality, one that she couldn't help but admire. Yet, even as her curiosity grew, a nagging sense of duty tugged at her mind, reminding her of the responsibilities that lay heavy on her shoulders.

Callista stepped back, her fingers absently tracing the cool stone of the temple wall. She knew she shouldn't linger or allow herself to be distracted by the enigmatic stranger. But there was something about him, a magnetic pull that she couldn't quite explain.

Lost in thought, Callista didn't notice the approach of Priestess Eirene until she felt a gentle hand on her shoulder. "Is everything alright, High Priestess?" Eirene asked, her voice soft with concern.

Startled, Callista quickly composed herself. "Yes, of course. I was just..." She trailed off, her gaze drifting back to where Dorian stood, now engrossed in the intricate frescoes adorning the temple walls.

Eirene followed her gaze, a knowing smile playing at the corners of her lips. "He seems to have made quite an impression on our people."

Callista nodded, her thoughts still swirling. "There's something different about him, something that sets him apart."

"Perhaps it's his openness, his willingness to embrace our ways," Eirene mused. "It's a rare quality in an outsider."

As they watched, Dorian turned, his eyes meeting Callista's across the expanse of the temple. For a fleeting moment, time seemed to still, and Callista felt a spark of connection, a whisper of something she couldn't quite name. She held his gaze, her heart quickening in her chest, before finally tearing her eyes away.

"I should go," she murmured, her voice barely above a whisper. "There are matters that require my attention."

Eirene nodded, her expression one of understanding. "Of course, High Priestess. But remember, even the most dedicated among us must allow ourselves moments of respite."

With a final glance in Dorian's direction, Callista slipped away, her mind awhirl with conflicting emotions. As she made her way deeper into the temple, she couldn't shake the feeling that her path was somehow intertwined with Dorian's, that their meeting was more than mere chance. It was a thought both thrilling and terrifying, one that she knew would linger long after she had returned to her duties.

Callista found solace in the familiar rhythms of her duties, the ancient rituals and sacred rites providing a much-needed anchor amidst the turbulent sea of her thoughts. She moved through the temple with practiced grace, her footsteps echoing softly against the stone floors as she tended to the altars and offerings.

Yet even as she went about her tasks, her mind remained fixed on the vision that had shaken her to her core. The flames, the trembling earth, the sense of impending doom all lingered in her consciousness, a constant reminder of the weight that rested upon her shoulders.

As she knelt before the statue of Potnia, her fingers tracing the well-worn contours of the stone, Callista closed her eyes and whispered a fervent prayer. "Great Mother, guide me in these uncertain times. Grant me the wisdom to interpret your signs and the strength to protect our people."

The flickering light of the oil lamps cast dancing shadows on the walls, and for a moment, Callista could almost feel the presence of the goddess. Her gentle warmth enveloped her like a comforting embrace.

But even as she drew strength from her faith, her thoughts drifted unbidden to Dorian, to the enigmatic stranger who had so easily captured the hearts of her people. She couldn't deny the pull she felt towards him, the inexplicable sense of connection that seemed to defy all reason.

Callista shook her head, chiding herself for allowing such thoughts to intrude upon her sacred duties. She was responsible to her people, a calling transcending personal desires or fleeting attractions.

And yet, as she rose to her feet and made her way towards the temple's inner sanctum, she couldn't help but wonder what the future might hold. The vision had shown her a world on the brink of chaos, a land consumed by fire and destruction. But perhaps, just perhaps, there was still hope to be found amidst the ashes.

Chapter 4: Wisdom of the Elders

Callista's fingers trailed along the ancient stone walls, tracing the intricate carvings and faded frescoes. Her sandals whispered against the worn floor as she followed Eirene deeper into the temple archives. The scent of frankincense and cedarwood enveloped them, a heady perfume that spoke of the sacred wisdom contained within these walls.

"I can almost hear the voices of the ancestors in this place," Callista murmured, her eyes shining with reverence. "Their knowledge echoes through the ages, waiting to be rediscovered."

Eirene smiled, her weathered face creasing with gentle understanding. "The archives hold many secrets, my dear. Some are meant for us to uncover, while others may yet remain hidden until the goddess deems us ready."

They approached the towering shelves, each one laden with meticulously organized scrolls. The soft flicker of oil lamps cast dancing shadows across the yellowed parchment as if the very words themselves were alive and breathing. Callista's gaze was drawn to one particular scroll, its edges worn and frayed by the passage of time.

She reached out, her fingertips hovering just above the ancient document. A thrill ran through her, a sense of destiny tugging at her heart. She glanced at Eirene, seeking guidance and permission.

The older priestess nodded, her eyes twinkling with a hint of mischief. "Go on, child. Let your instincts guide you. The goddess often speaks to us through the subtle whispers of our own curiosity."

With a deep breath, Callista gently lifted the scroll from its resting place. The weight of it in her hands felt both familiar and profound as if she were holding a piece of history itself. She carried it to a nearby table, her heart racing with anticipation.

As she carefully unrolled the delicate parchment, Callista couldn't help but wonder what secrets lay hidden within the faded ink and ancient symbols. What wisdom of the ancients would be revealed to her today? And how might it shape the path that lay ahead?

Eirene's comforting presence at her side steadied her nerves. Together, they leaned in to study the scroll, their heads bowed in shared reverence and curiosity. The soft rustle of parchment and the quiet murmur of their voices filled the archives, a sacred moment of discovery unfolding in the heart of the temple.

As Callista's eyes scanned the ancient text, her brow furrowed in concentration. The faded ink spoke of past calamities, of the earth shaking and the seas rising, of the goddess Potnia's fury unleashed upon the land. The words seemed to dance before her, a haunting testament to the fragility of their world.

"The Great Mother's wrath is not to be taken lightly," Callista murmured, her finger tracing a line of text. "It says here that the people of old failed to honor her, and the consequences were dire."

Eirene leaned closer, her silver hair brushing against Callista's shoulder. "Ah, yes. The tale of the forgotten offerings. I remember my own mentor speaking of this when I was a young acolyte."

Callista turned to her, curiosity sparkling in her green eyes. "What happened?"

"The story goes that the people of another of Potnia's great cities grew complacent, taking for granted the bounty the goddess provided. They neglected their duties, their offerings becoming mere afterthoughts." Eirene's voice took on a storyteller's cadence, her words painting vivid pictures in the air between them.

"Potnia's anger grew, as hot as the forges of Vulkan, the demi-god bronze smith, himself. The earth began to tremble, the skies darkened, and the seas churned with her rage. The people, realizing their folly, fell to their knees in desperate prayer."

Callista's heart raced, the weight of responsibility pressing upon her. "What did they do? How did they appease her?"

Eirene's blue eyes met hers, a flicker of understanding passing between them. "They remembered, child. They remembered the old ways, they took to the sea and made their way to a new home as their city, a great work of their hubris was swallowed by ash and the tides. They came together as one in a virgin land, offering their most precious gifts to the Mother, pouring their hearts into their prayers."

She reached out, her hand resting gently on Callista's arm. "And in that moment of unity, of genuine faith, Potnia's anger cooled and she blessed their new home with an abundance.. Balance was restored."

Callista nodded, her mind whirling with the implications of the tale. She glanced back at the scroll, a newfound appreciation for the wisdom it contained. "We must never forget," she whispered, more to herself than to Eirene. "We must always honor the Mother, in all we do."

Eirene smiled, a knowing look in her eyes. "And that, my dear, is the key to harmony. To remember our place in the tapestry of the world, to give as much as we receive, and to always keep the sacred fires burning bright."

As they carefully rolled the scroll, securing it with a soft leather tie, Callista felt a renewed sense of purpose settle over her. The weight of her duties felt less like a burden and more like a sacred trust, a chance to guide her people along the path of righteousness.

She turned to Eirene, gratitude shining in her eyes. "Thank you, Eirene. For your wisdom, your guidance, and your friendship. I am truly blessed to have you by my side."

The older priestess chuckled softly, her laughter like the tinkling of wind chimes. "Oh, my dear Callista. It is I who am blessed. To witness the blossoming of a true leader, a woman of faith and courage? That is a gift beyond measure."

They left the archives for now, and as they stepped into the temple courtyard, the warm sun caressed Callista's face. A gentle breeze carried the sweet scent of blooming jasmine. The world seemed to hold its breath as if waiting for her to take the next step on her journey.

Eirene placed a comforting hand on Callista's shoulder. "The path of a high priestess is not an easy one, my dear. It is a road paved with sacrifice and devotion. But it is also a path of great joy and fulfillment."

Callista nodded, her eyes fixed on the distant horizon. "I know there is much I still have to learn, Eirene. About our traditions, our people, and about myself. But I am ready to embrace this journey, to let it shape me into the leader Potnia knows I can be."

"And what of your own desires, Callista?" Eirene asked gently. "What of the yearnings of your heart?"

Callista's breath caught in her throat. How could Eirene know the longing that stirred within her? The desire to explore, to experience, to taste the world beyond the sacred bounds of Thera? The desire for companionship.

"I... I know my duty lies here, Eirene. With our people, with our goddess. But sometimes..." She trailed off, her gaze drifting to the distant sea.

Eirene squeezed her shoulder, a knowing smile on her lips. "It is natural to wonder, my dear. To dream of what lies beyond our shores. But remember, true fulfillment comes from embracing the role the Fates have spun for us. Whatever that may be"

Callista sighed, her heart a battleground of conflicting desires. "I know, Eirene. I just... I cannot help but feel that there is more to this life than what lies within these temple walls."

"And perhaps there is, my dear. But for now, your path is here. To lead, to guide, to serve. Trust in Potnia's wisdom, and she will not lead you astray. She may even lead what you need and desire right to you!"

With a final squeeze of her shoulder, Eirene turned and walked back into the temple, leaving Callista alone with her thoughts. She knew her mentor was right. Her place was here, her duty to her people and her goddess.

But as she stood there, the sun warm on her skin and the breeze whispering secrets in her ear, she couldn't shake the feeling that her journey was only just beginning. Her destiny was waiting to be discovered somewhere out there, beyond the horizon.

The next day, the vibrant hues of the marketplace danced before Callista's eyes as she wandered through the bustling stalls. Crimson fabrics fluttered in the breeze, their intricate patterns catching the sunlight, while baskets overflowed with ripe fruits and fragrant herbs. The air was alive with the chatter of merchants and the laughter of children, a symphony of life that filled her senses.

A rich voice caught her attention as she paused to examine a delicate silver bracelet, her fingers tracing the intricate engravings. The voice commanded the crowd, weaving tales of distant lands and epic adventures. Callista turned, her curiosity piqued, and found herself drawn to the source of the captivating words.

There, in the center of a small gathering, stood a man unlike any she had seen before. His sun-bronzed skin and wind-tousled hair spoke of a life spent at sea, while his vibrant blue eyes sparkled with mischief and wonder. He gestured animatedly as he spoke, his words painting vivid pictures in the minds of his listeners. As she got closer, she realized she had seen him before. It was Dorian!

"And there I was, standing at the edge of the world, the endless expanse of the ocean stretching out before me," he said, his voice low and conspiratorial. "The salty spray kissed my face as the wind whispered secrets of lands yet undiscovered. It was in that moment, my friends, that I knew my journey had only just begun."

The crowd hung on his every word, their eyes wide with wonder. Callista found herself inching closer, drawn in by the magnetic pull of his presence. As she listened, she felt a stirring in her heart, a yearning for the freedom and adventure his tales promised.

"Excuse me," she said softly, her voice barely audible above the din of the marketplace. "Might I ask your name, traveler?"

The man turned, his eyes meeting hers, and with a coy smile, he played along. "Dorian," he said, a warm smile spreading across his face. "Dorian Xenophon, at your service, my lady."

Callista felt a flush rise to her cheeks as she returned his smile, happy to be playing this game together. "Callista Antheia," she replied, dipping her head in greeting. "Your stories... they are unlike anything I have ever heard before. The way you speak of the world beyond our shores, it is truly captivating."

Dorian's grin widened, his eyes crinkling at the corners. "Ah, but the world is full of wonders, High Priestess. Wonders that words can scarcely do justice. To truly understand, one must experience them firsthand."

He leaned in closer, his voice dropping to a conspiratorial whisper. "Tell me, Callista Antheia, have you ever dreamed of setting sail? Of leaving behind the familiar and embracing the unknown?"

Callista's heart raced at his words, the yearning in her soul growing stronger with each passing moment. Glancing back toward the temple, its white walls gleaming in the distance, she turned to meet Dorian's gaze once more.

"I... I have duties here," she said, her voice trembling slightly. "Responsibilities to my people, to my goddess. But..." She paused, taking a deep breath. "But I would be lying if I said I did not long for something more. Something beyond the confines of this island."

Dorian's eyes softened, understanding etched across his features. "It is a difficult balance, is it not? Between duty and desire, between the known and the unknown."

He reached out, his fingers brushing against her arm in a gesture of reassurance. "But know this, Callista Antheia. The world will wait for you. And when the time is right, when your heart is ready... it will be there, waiting to welcome you with open arms. For the only thing that will always outlive us, is the earth."

With those words, he turned back to the crowd, his voice rising once more as he launched into another tale of adventure. But as Callista watched him, her mind swirling with possibilities, she knew that his words would linger long after the marketplace had emptied.

For in that moment, a seed had been planted in her heart. A seed of wanderlust, of curiosity, of longing. And though she knew her path was here, in the service of her goddess and her people, she couldn't help but wonder what the future might hold.

Callista remained at the edge of the gathering, her eyes still fixed on Dorian as he wove another tale, his voice painting vivid pictures of distant shores and exotic cultures. She marveled at his ability to captivate the audience, to draw them in with each carefully chosen word.

As she listened, her mind wandered to the ancient scrolls she had studied in the temple archives. The tales of brave heroes and their epic journeys, of the challenges they faced and the triumphs they achieved. In Dorian's stories, she found echoes of those legends, a connection to a world she had only ever experienced through the written word.

The crowd hung on Dorian's every word, their eyes wide with wonder as he described the towering waves of a storm-tossed sea, the glittering spires of a far-off city, the sweet fragrance of a foreign blossom. Callista found herself leaning forward, eager to catch every detail, every nuance of his story.

And then, as his tale reached its climax, Dorian's voice rose to a crescendo. He spoke of a daring escape, a narrow victory against impossible odds, and the crowd erupted in applause. Callista joined them, her own hands coming together in a gesture of appreciation and admiration.

As the applause died down, Dorian's eyes found hers once more. In that moment, a silent understanding passed between them. A recognition of the power of stories, of the way they could transport the listener to another time and place.

Callista felt a smile tug at the corners of her lips, a reflection of the warmth and camaraderie that flowed through the marketplace. She knew that this moment, this connection, would stay with her long after the day had ended.

For in Dorian's tales, she had found a glimpse of the wider world. A world full of wonder and possibility, of adventure and discovery. And though her duties to Potnia and her people anchored her to Thera, she knew that a part of her would always long to explore those distant horizons.

When Dorian was finished telling the locals his stories he and Callista stopped their game of pretending to have just met and moved through the marketplace together. Callista found herself drawn to his interactions with the locals. He approached each stall with genuine curiosity, asking questions about the wares and the stories behind them. The vendors, charmed by his interest and easy smile, eagerly shared their knowledge, their faces lighting up with pride as they spoke of their crafts.

Dorian listened intently, his eyes sparkling with appreciation for the artistry and skill on display. He examined a delicately woven tapestry, running his fingers over the intricate patterns. "This is exquisite," he marveled, turning to the weaver. "How long did it take you to create such a masterpiece?"

The weaver, a weathered old woman with a twinkle in her eye, chuckled softly. "Oh, it's a labor of love, my dear. Each thread holds a piece of my heart, a memory of the stories passed down through generations."

Dorian's smile widened, his admiration evident. "And it shows, in every stitch. Your work is a testament to the rich history and culture of Thera."

As he continued through the market, Dorian's laughter rang out, a melody that seemed to weave itself into the very fabric of the bustling scene. It was infectious, spreading from stall to stall, until the entire marketplace seemed to pulse with a shared joy.

Callista, felt her heart flutter with a mix of emotions. She knew she should return to her duties, to the sacred responsibilities that awaited her at the temple. And yet, the allure of Dorian's presence, the way he seemed to bring life and color to everything around him, was a temptation she found difficult to resist.

"What am I doing?" she whispered to herself, her fingers absently twisting the sacred ribbons that adorned her hair. "I am the High Priestess of Potnia, bound by duty and tradition. I cannot allow myself to be swept away by a stranger's charms, no matter how compelling they may be."

And yet, even as the words left her lips, Callista knew that something had changed within her. The spark of excitement that Dorian's stories had ignited, the longing for adventure and discovery that his presence seemed to awaken – these were not things she could easily ignore. Callista excused herself from Dorian quickly, who was clearly upset by her quick departure but smiled warmly nonetheless. “Of course High Priestess, I am sure you have much to attend to. But my whole hearted thanks to you for keeping me company in the market today.”

As the last rays of the sun painted the sky in hues of gold and crimson, Callista ascended the steps of the Temple of Potnia, her footfalls echoing softly against the ancient stone. The familiar scent of incense and the gentle rustling of her robes provided a small measure of comfort, but her mind remained a tempest of conflicting emotions.

She paused at the entrance, her hand resting on the intricately carved doorframe. The weight of her responsibilities settled upon her shoulders like a mantle, a reminder of the path she had chosen so long ago. And yet, the events of the day had awakened something within her – a yearning for something more, a desire to explore the world beyond the confines of her sacred duties.

"Callista?" a soft voice called from within the temple. "Is everything alright?"

Callista turned to see Eirene, her trusted acolyte, emerging from the shadows. The concern in the woman's eyes was evident, a reflection of the bond they shared.

"I am fine, Eirene," Callista replied, forcing a smile. "Just lost in thought, I suppose."

Eirene nodded, her gaze searching. "You seem troubled, High Priestess. Is there anything I can do to help?"

Callista hesitated, the urge to confide in her friend warring with her need to maintain the image of strength and composure that her position demanded. "I... I find myself questioning things, Eirene. Things I have always taken for granted."

Eirene's eyes widened, but she remained silent, allowing Callista to continue.

"Meeting up with Dorian today in the marketplace, hearing his stories... it stirred something within me. A longing for adventure, for a life beyond the temple walls." Callista's voice was barely above a whisper, as though speaking the words aloud made them more real, more dangerous.

Eirene reached out, placing a comforting hand on Callista's arm. "It is only natural to feel this way, Callista. We are all human, with desires and dreams of our own. But you must remember the importance of your role, the trust that Potnia has placed in you. You may find that her desires for you, and yours for yourself, may not be that different in the end."

Callista nodded, her heart heavy with the truth of Eirene's words. "I know, my friend. I know. But how do I reconcile these feelings with my duty in the moment? How do I find peace when my heart is torn in two?"

Eirene smiled, her eyes shining with wisdom beyond her years. "By trusting in Potnia's guidance, and in your own strength. You have faced challenges before, Callista, and emerged stronger for them. This, too, shall pass."

Callista drew a deep breath, allowing Eirene's words to wash over her like a soothing balm. "Thank you, Eirene. Your friendship means more to me than you know." As the two women entered the temple, the golden glow of the setting sun giving way to the flickering light of the torches, Callista felt a renewed sense of purpose. The path ahead might be uncertain, but she knew that with the support of her loved ones and the guidance of Potnia, she would find her way.

Callista's footsteps echoed softly against the stone floor as she made her way through the temple's dimly lit corridors. The day's encounters swirled in her mind, a kaleidoscope of emotions and possibilities. She paused before a statue of Potnia, the goddess's serene face illuminated by the gentle flicker of a nearby torch.

"Oh, great Potnia," Callista whispered, her voice a delicate thread in the stillness of the night. "I seek your guidance in these uncertain times. My heart is torn between duty and desire, and I fear the path ahead."

She closed her eyes, her hands clasped in silent prayer. The scent of incense lingered in the air, a subtle reminder of the sacred rituals that had shaped her life. As she stood there, lost in thought, a gentle breeze stirred the air, carrying with it the distant sound of the sea.

Callista's eyes fluttered open, a soft gasp escaping her lips. The statue seemed to glow with an otherworldly light, its features shimmering like starlight against the darkness. She reached out, her fingertips grazing the cool stone, and felt a surge of energy coursing through her veins.

"I understand, my lady," she murmured, her voice trembling with newfound resolve. "Change is inevitable, a part of the great cycle of life. I must embrace it, even if it means facing the unknown."

With a final bow of reverence, Callista turned away from the statue, her steps lighter than before. She made her way to her chambers, the weight of her responsibilities no longer a burden, but a source of strength.

As she lay down to rest, the gentle sound of the waves lulling her to sleep, Callista knew that whatever challenges lay ahead, she would face them with the grace and courage that Potnia had bestowed upon her. The future was uncertain, but in that moment, she found solace in the knowledge that she was exactly where she was meant to be.

Chapter 5: Echoes of the Past

The fragrant smoke of frankincense curled lazily around Callista as she lit the morning candles, her slender fingers steady and sure. The familiar scent filled her nostrils, transporting her back to her early days as an acolyte in the Temple of Potnia. Even then, the weight of her future responsibilities had pressed upon her young shoulders.

A slight smile played at the corners of her lips as the memory took hold, carrying her back to a time when the towering stone columns of the temple seemed to dwarf her small frame. She could still feel the cool marble beneath her feet and hear the gentle rustling of her simple linen tunic.

***

"Callista, concentrate," came the stern voice of her mentor, Priestess Thalia. The older woman's keen eyes missed nothing as she observed the girl's efforts to master the sacred chants. "From the beginning, child."

Taking a deep breath, Callista straightened her posture and began anew, her high, clear voice ringing out in the hushed chamber. With each repetition, her words grew stronger and more confident, echoing off the ancient walls.

"Mother Potnia, hear our prayer, guide us with your wisdom fair," she intoned, losing herself in the hypnotic rhythm of the chant. "Bless our land with fertile soil, protect us from strife and toil."

As the final notes faded, Callista met her mentor's gaze, seeking approval in those deep, knowing eyes. Thalia's face softened, a rare smile gracing her weathered features.

"Well done, my dear," she said, resting a gentle hand on the girl's shoulder. "The Great Mother has surely heard your devotion today."

Callista beamed with pride, basking in the warmth of her mentor's praise. In that moment, the challenges that lay ahead seemed surmountable, her path as a priestess of Potnia stretching out before her like a shining thread of destiny.

The scent of frankincense grew stronger, pulling Callista back to the present. She blinked, the temple coming into focus once more. The weight of her responsibilities settled upon her like a familiar cloak, but she wore it with grace and confidence, secure in the knowledge that her years of dedication had prepared her well for the role of High Priestess.

***

The bustling marketplace of Kition, Cyprus, hummed with life as Dorian weaved his way through the colorful stalls. The air was heavy with the mingled scents of cinnamon, saffron, and freshly baked bread, while the clamor of merchants haggling and friends laughing filled his ears. His eyes sparkled with youthful curiosity, and he was eager to absorb every detail of the vibrant scene.

"Dorian, my boy!" A booming voice caught his attention. "Come, see what treasures I've brought from the East!"

Grinning, Dorian approached the stall of his favorite trader, Demetrios. The old man's weathered face crinkled with a smile as he gestured to an array of exotic spices and gleaming trinkets.

"Ah, Demetrios, you never fail to impress," Dorian chuckled, picking up a small brass compass. "What stories do these hold?"

As Demetrios launched into a tale of far-off lands and daring adventures, Dorian's gaze wandered, settling on a striking young woman across the marketplace. Her raven hair cascaded down her back, and her olive skin glowed in the afternoon sun. As if sensing his stare, she turned, her dark eyes meeting his with an intensity that stole his breath.

"Who is she?" Dorian whispered, unable to tear his gaze away.

Demetrios followed his line of sight, a knowing smile playing on his lips. "That, my boy, is Lyra, the daughter of a wealthy merchant. But be warned, her father guards her like a dragon hoards gold."

Dorian barely heard him, his heart pounding as Lyra offered him a shy smile before disappearing into the crowd. At that moment, he knew his life would never be the same.

***

Under the canopy of stars, Dorian and Lyra lay entwined in a hidden cove, the soft lapping of waves against the shore had been a gentle accompaniment to their rhythmic movements earlier. Dorian traced the delicate line of her jaw, marveling at the softness of her skin.

"I want nothing more than to spend my life with you," he murmured, his voice thick with emotion. "To wake each morning to your smile and fall asleep each night with you in my arms."

Lyra's eyes shimmered with unshed tears, her fingers lacing with his. "And I with you, my love. We'll build a life together, filled with laughter and adventure, no matter what challenges we face."

They sealed their vow with a tender kiss, the stars above bearing witness to their love. But even as they lost themselves in the sweetness of the moment, the distant call of the sea tugged at Dorian's heart, a reminder of the life he had always known.

***

The day of their parting dawned gray and cold, the wind whipping at their clothes as they stood on the dock. Dorian held Lyra close, memorizing the feel of her in his arms, the scent of her hair, the sound of her heartbeat.

"I will return to you," he promised, his voice cracking with emotion. "No matter how long it takes, no matter what storms I must weather, I will find my way back to you."

Lyra clung to him, her tears mingling with the salt spray on her cheeks. "I will wait for you, my love. Forever, if I must."

With a final, desperate kiss, Dorian tore himself away, his feet heavy as he boarded the waiting ship. As the vessel pulled away from the dock, he kept his eyes fixed on Lyra's diminishing form, her hand raised in a silent farewell. The ache in his chest grew with each passing moment, the realization that he was leaving behind his heart, his future, his everything.

As Cyprus faded into the horizon, Dorian steeled himself against the pain, focusing on the promise of return. He would come back to her, no matter the cost. But for now, the sea called, and he had no choice but to answer.

***

The gentle rustling of parchment filled the temple's library as Callista traced her fingers along the edges of an ancient scroll. Lost in thought, she marveled at the wisdom contained within the delicate papyrus, a treasure trove of divine knowledge passed down through generations of high priestesses.

A distant rumble, like the growl of a slumbering beast, shattered her concentration. Callista's eyes widened as the ground beneath her feet trembled, the shelves around her groaning in protest. She steadied herself against the table, her heart racing as the unsettling vibrations subsided.

"The earth grows restless," she murmured, a frown creasing her brow. "Potnia, guide us through these uncertain times."

Across the island, in the bustling coastal settlement of Akrotiri, Theron navigated the temple's sun-drenched courtyard. His dusty robes swirled around his ankles as he walked, his mind preoccupied with the recent tremors that seemed to grow more frequent with each passing day.

As he passed the central fountain, Theron's thoughts drifted to his first encounter with Callista, the high priestess whose presence had captivated him from the moment he laid eyes on her. He remembered the way she stood amidst the crowd of worshippers, her ethereal beauty and quiet strength drawing him in like a moth to a flame.

"Brother Theron!" a young acolyte called out, jolting him from his reverie. "The scrolls you requested have arrived from Pyrgos Kallistis."

Theron smiled, nodding his thanks to the eager youth. "Excellent. I shall review them in my study. If you'll excuse me..."

As he made his way towards the temple archives, Theron couldn't shake the image of Callista from his mind. He knew it was foolish to harbor such thoughts, but there was something about her that stirred his soul in ways he had never experienced before.

"Focus, Theron," he chided himself, shaking his head as he entered the cool, shadowed confines of the archive. "There are more pressing matters at hand."

With a sigh, he unrolled the first scroll, his eyes scanning the ancient text for any clues that might shed light on the island's increasingly unstable nature. As he delved deeper into his research, Theron couldn't help but wonder if Callista, too, was searching for answers, her own thoughts consumed by the ominous rumblings that echoed through the very heart of Thera.

***

In the heart of the temple complex, Callista sat across from Priestess Eirene, her brow furrowed with concern. "The tremors grow more frequent and intense with each passing day," she said softly, her fingers absently tracing the intricate patterns embroidered on her robes. "I fear for the safety of our people, Eirene. What do the omens tell you?"

Eirene's gentle blue eyes met Callista's, a flicker of uncertainty passing between them. "The signs are... unclear," she admitted, her voice barely above a whisper. "The earth speaks in riddles, and the smoke from our offerings twists in strange patterns. I have sought guidance from Potnia herself, but her message remains veiled."

Callista nodded, her heart heavy with the weight of their shared responsibility. "We must be vigilant," she said, her voice steady despite the unease that gripped her. "Our people look to us for guidance and protection. We cannot fail them."

As if in response to her words, the ground beneath their feet suddenly heaved, sending tremors racing through the temple walls. Callista and Eirene braced themselves against the marble table, their eyes wide with fear as the ancient stones groaned and shuddered around them.

"Potnia, protect us," Eirene whispered, her fingers clutching the sacred amulet that hung from her neck.

Callista's mind raced, her thoughts turning to the countless lives that depended on their leadership. She knew that they could not afford to falter, not when the very foundations of their world were being shaken to the core. As the tremors subsided, leaving an eerie silence in their wake, Callista rose to her feet, her resolve hardening like tempered steel. "We must consult the ancient texts again," she said, her voice ringing with authority. "There must be more wisdom hidden within their pages, secrets that could help us navigate these troubled times."

Eirene nodded, her own determination mirroring Callista's. "I will gather the acolytes and begin the search at once. With Potnia's guidance, we will find a way to protect our people and preserve the sacred traditions of Thera."

As the two women set about their task, their footsteps echoing through the hallowed halls of the temple, Callista's thoughts briefly turned to Theron, the young priest whose curious mind and gentle spirit had captured her attention. She wondered if he, too, was searching for answers, his own path intertwined with the fate of their beloved island.

With a silent prayer to Potnia, Callista pushed aside her personal musings, focusing instead on the enormous responsibility that lay ahead. The future of Thera hung in the balance, and she would stop at nothing to ensure the survival and prosperity of her people.

***

Chaos erupted within the temple as another violent tremor shook the sacred ground. Acolytes and villagers alike scrambled to secure the precious artifacts, their voices rising in a cacophony of fear and determination.

Amidst the turmoil, Callista's voice rang out, clear and commanding. "Quickly, move the sacred scrolls to the inner sanctuary!" She gestured towards a group of young acolytes, her eyes intense with purpose. "And you, gather the ceremonial vessels and take them to the underground chambers."

The acolytes sprang into action, their movements swift and precise, guided by Callista's unwavering leadership. She moved among them, her presence a beacon of calm in the chaos, offering words of encouragement and direction.

"Remember, we are the guardians of Potnia's sacred mysteries," Callista called out, her voice carrying above the din. "We must protect her treasures, no matter the cost."

As the last of the artifacts were secured, Callista turned to Eirene, her trusted companion. "Ensure the villagers who travelled here for guidance are safely sheltered within the temple walls. I will make an offering to Potnia, seeking her guidance and protection."

Eirene nodded, her eyes reflecting the gravity of the situation. "May the Great Mother watch over us all," she murmured, hurrying off to gather the frightened villagers.

Callista made her way to the altar, her steps measured and purposeful. As she knelt before the sacred flame, her thoughts drifted to the challenges that lay ahead. "Great Potnia," she whispered, her voice fervent with devotion, "grant us the strength and wisdom to navigate these troubled times. Guide us, your faithful servants, as we seek to preserve the sacred mysteries of Thera."

As the tremors subsided, Callista rose from her prayer, her resolve fortified by her unwavering faith. She knew that the path ahead would be fraught with trials, but with Potnia's blessing and the strength of her people, they would weather the storm together.

Miles away, along the rugged coastline of Thera, Dorian found himself caught in the midst of the earth's violent upheaval. The ground beneath his feet shifted and roiled, sending him stumbling as he fought to maintain his balance.

"By the gods!" he exclaimed, his eyes widening as he watched boulders tumble from the cliffs above, crashing into the churning sea below.

Dorian's mind raced with memories of past adventures, of storms weathered and challenges overcome. Yet none had prepared him for the raw power of the earth itself, the primal force that now threatened to tear the very island asunder. He remembered with a deep sadness, the violent tremor, and rushing tides, that Demetrius had told him pulled his beloved Lyra out to her watery grave.

As he struggled to find stable footing, Dorian's thoughts turned to the people of Thera, to the vibrant communities and sacred traditions that had captured his heart. He knew that he could not stand idly by while the island and its inhabitants faced such peril. His eyes filled with tears as his heart sank, looking at this island, so similar to his own, and these people who might suffer a fate similar to his Lyra.

With a determined set to his jaw, Dorian began to make his way back towards the heart of the island, his steps uneasy but unwavering. He knew not what challenges lay ahead, but he was certain of one thing: he would stand with the people of Thera, offering his strength and support in their time of need.

* * *

In his personal study, Theron worked feverishly, his hands shaking as he gathered the fallen scrolls. The tremor had sent the ancient texts tumbling from their shelves, scattering them across the stone floor like leaves in the wind.

As he reached for another scroll, Theron's eyes fell upon a faded inscription, the words nearly lost to time. His heart pounded with a sudden urgency as he read the cryptic message, his mind racing to decipher its meaning.

"The earth shall tremble," he murmured, his voice barely audible above the distant rumble of the tremors. "The sea shall rise, and the sky shall weep tears of fire."

With trembling fingers, Theron unrolled the scroll further, his eyes scanning the text for any clue, any hint of what was to come. The ancient words spoke of a great calamity, a time when the very foundations of the world would be shaken. As he read on, Theron's heart sank with a growing sense of dread. The scrolls spoke of a powerful force, a primal energy that lay dormant beneath the earth. It was a force that could not be harnessed, it could not be abated, it could not be quelled.

Theron's mind raced with the implications of his discovery. If the ancient texts were to be believed, then the tremors were only the beginning. The island of Thera was in grave danger, its very existence threatened by a power beyond their understanding. With a sense of grim determination, Theron gathered the scrolls, his movements precise and purposeful. He knew that he had to bring this information to Callista, to the high priestess who held the fate of Thera in her hands.

As he hurried from his study, Theron couldn't shake the feeling that time was running out. The earth continued to tremble beneath his feet, a constant reminder of the danger that lurked beneath the surface.

But even as fear gripped his heart, Theron found himself clinging to a glimmer of hope. The ancient texts had spoken of a great calamity, yes, but they had also hinted at a path forward, a of a people escaping to better lands and Potnia's grace.

It was a path fraught with peril, a road that would test the very limits of their faith and their strength. But as Theron emerged into the fading light of day, he knew it was a path they had no choice but to follow.

The fate of Thera hung in the balance, and with it, the lives of all who called the island home. As Theron made his way towards the heart of the temple, he silently prayed to the gods for guidance, for the strength to face whatever challenges lay ahead.

For in the end, he knew that it would be the power of their faith, the unbreakable bonds of their community, that would see them through the darkness and into the light beyond.

***

As the sun dipped below the horizon, painting the sky in hues of orange and pink, Callista stood atop the temple steps, her gaze fixed on the distant sea. The tremors had subsided, but the unease that had settled over the island remained, a palpable presence that hung heavy in the air.

She closed her eyes, allowing the salty breeze to caress her face, and drew in a deep, steadying breath. The weight of her responsibilities pressed down upon her, a burden that seemed to grow heavier with each passing day.

"The gods are testing us," a familiar voice said from behind her.

Callista turned to see Dorian approaching, his windswept hair and sun-bronzed skin a testament to the hours he had spent helping the fishermen secure their boats.

"And we must not be found wanting," Callista replied, her voice steady despite the turmoil that raged within her.

Dorian came to stand beside her, his gaze following hers out to sea. "The people are afraid," he said softly. "They look to you for guidance, for reassurance."

Callista nodded, the beads in her hair clinking softly with the movement. "I know," she whispered. "But what reassurance can I offer when I myself am so uncertain?"

Dorian placed a gentle hand on her shoulder, his touch a comforting warmth in the cooling evening air. "You are not alone in this, Callista," he said firmly. "We will face whatever comes together, as a community, as a people."

As if on cue, Theron crossed the Temple threshold, his arms laden with ancient scrolls and texts. His face was etched with a mixture of excitement and trepidation as he hurried towards them.

"I think I've found something," he said breathlessly, his eyes shining with a feverish intensity. "A truth about the mountain and these quakes, perhaps a way to protect ourselves from the calamity that threatens to engulf us."

Callista and Dorian exchanged a glance, "Theron?" Callista asked.

Theron nodded, looking from Callista to Dorian. "This is Dorian, he is from Cyprus." Callista said as a way of introduction—the two clasped forearms in greeting.

"As I said, I think I found something."

Callist and Dorian both felt their hearts quickening with a sudden surge of hope. "Show us," Callista said, her voice thrumming with newfound determination.

As the three of them bent their heads over the ancient texts, the last rays of the setting sun bathed them in a golden glow, a fleeting moment of peace amidst the gathering storm. But even as they pored over the scrolls, their minds racing with possibilities and plans, a sense of foreboding hung heavy in the air, a whisper of the challenges ahead. For the fate of Thera and the lives of all who called it home now rested in their hands, a burden that they could not, would not, bear alone.

Chapter 6: Allies in Uncertainty

Callista stood at the head of the large, rectangular stone table in the temple's meeting chamber. Her dark hair, adorned with sacred ribbons and beads, framed her serene face as her green eyes surveyed the gathered council members. She took a deep breath, letting the salty sea breeze that wafted through the open windows fill her lungs.

"Thank you all for coming," she began, her voice steady and authoritative. "As you know, our beloved island of Thera has been experiencing unusual tremors as of late. It is urgent that we address this matter and determine the best course of action for the safety and well-being of our people."

Callista's words hung in the air, the gravity of the situation evident in the solemn expressions of those seated around the table. Yet her composed demeanor seemed to radiate a calming energy, setting the tone for the gathering.

A hand shot up eagerly, belonging to Ariadne Nereida, a young priestess with fiery red curls peeking out from beneath her white temple veil. Callista nodded in her direction, a faint smile tugging at the corners of her mouth. The girl's enthusiasm was palpable, even in the face of such dire circumstances.

"High Priestess Callista," Ariadne began, her brown eyes sparkling with intensity, "the fishermen have noticed strange happenings in the sea. They say the waters churn like a boiling pot, and the fish dart about as if Poseidon himself were chasing them with his mighty trident!"

A murmur rippled through the council at Ariadne's vivid description. Callista leaned forward slightly, intrigued by the young acolyte's report. The girl's informal speech and maritime metaphors painted a clear picture of the unease felt by the island's fishing community.

Callista's thoughts drifted briefly to her own childhood memories of watching the fishing boats return at sunset, their sails painted gold by the fading light. She understood the deep connection the people of Thera had with the sea, and how any disturbance in its rhythms could signal impending troubles.

"Thank you, Ariadne," Callista said warmly, her voice drawing the council's attention back to the matter at hand. "Your insights from the fishing community are invaluable. It is clear that these tremors are not only affecting the land but also the sea. We must consider all aspects of life on Thera as we seek to understand and address this threat."

As the council members nodded in agreement, Callista felt a flicker of hope amidst the uncertainty. With the collective wisdom and diverse perspectives of those gathered, she believed they could find a way to protect their sacred island and its people from the looming danger.

Captain Minoas Lysandros leaned forward, his weathered hands resting on the cool stone of the table. His dark eyes, sharp as a hawk's, surveyed the council before he spoke. "If I may, High Priestess," he began, his deep voice carrying the cadence of the sea, "I believe we must consider the possibility of evacuation."

The room fell silent, the weight of his words settling over the gathered council like a heavy fog. Minoas continued, undeterred by the somber atmosphere. "I've spent my life navigating the waters surrounding Thera, and I know every cove, every current, and every safe harbor. If the tremors continue to worsen, we may need to relocate our people to ensure their safety."

He paused, allowing his words to sink in before offering a pragmatic assessment. "The western coast of the island has several deep-water ports that could accommodate our fishing vessels and merchant ships, besides the capital itself. From there, we could establish routes to the mainland or to neighboring islands, depending on the severity of the situation."

Callista nodded thoughtfully, her green eyes meeting Minoas' steady gaze. "Your expertise is greatly appreciated, Captain. We must indeed prepare for all eventualities, and your knowledge of our maritime capabilities will be essential in crafting an effective evacuation plan."

Seated beside Callista, Dorian Xenophon listened intently, his brow furrowed in concentration. As Minoas concluded his assessment, Dorian leaned forward, his voice warm and engaging. "If I may add to the captain's insights," he began, a hint of a smile playing at the corners of his mouth, "during my travels, I've learned much about how other lands have dealt with similar crises."

He wove a tale of a distant city, nestled in the shadow of a great mountain, much like Thera. "When the earth began to tremble and the mountain spewed ash and smoke, the people of that city formed alliances with their neighbors. Together, they created a network of support, sharing resources and knowledge to ensure the safety of all."

Dorian's eyes sparkled with enthusiasm as he continued, "Perhaps we could learn from their example and reach out to your allies. The bonds we forge in times of crisis may not only help you navigate this current challenge but also strengthen Thera's position in the years to come."

Callista felt a surge of gratitude for Dorian's diplomatic insights. His ability to draw upon the experiences of other lands and suggest creative solutions was a valuable asset to the council. She couldn't help but admire the way his charisma and intellect seemed to illuminate even the darkest of discussions.

As the council members murmured their agreement, Callista's thoughts turned to the monumental task ahead. Evacuating an entire island would require careful planning, cooperation, and the wisdom of all those gathered. But with Minoas' maritime expertise, Dorian's diplomatic savvy, and the collective strength of the council, she felt a glimmer of hope amidst the gathering storm.

The heavy wooden doors of the chamber creaked open, drawing the attention of the gathered council members. Theron Stavros strode into the room, his lean frame wrapped in simple temple robes, a satchel filled with observation tools slung across his shoulder. A ripple of tension passed through the council as he approached the stone table, his ink-stained fingers brushing against the ancient surface.

Theron's thoughtful brown eyes met Callista's piercing green gaze, a silent acknowledgment of the rivalry that had long existed between their temples. Yet, as he spoke, his voice carried a quiet authority that demanded attention. "I come before you today not as a rival, but as a fellow servant of Thera," he began, his words carefully chosen. "The tremors that shake our island threaten us all, regardless of the gods we serve. In this time of crisis, we must set aside our differences and work together for the greater good of our people."

Dorian leaned back in his seat, his warm smile faltering slightly as he studied Theron with a mix of curiosity and reservation. The young temple priest's precise speech and reverent tone stood in stark contrast to Dorian's own easy eloquence and adventurous spirit. As the discussion unfolded, subtle glances and pointed remarks passed between the two men, a testament to the underlying friction that simmered beneath the surface.

"Your observations of the mountain's activity are valuable, Theron," Dorian acknowledged, his voice tinged with a hint of skepticism. "But we must also consider the practical implications of an evacuation. The lives of our people cannot be entrusted to faith alone."

Theron's eyes narrowed slightly, his ink-stained fingers tightening around the edge of the table. "Faith and reason are not mutually exclusive, Dorian. The gods have granted us the wisdom to interpret the signs before us, and the courage to act upon that knowledge."

As the two men continued to exchange barbs, Callista felt a growing sense of unease.

Callista's thoughts raced as she watched the tension between Theron and Dorian unfold. She knew that their ability to work together would be crucial in the days to come, and she silently prayed to the gods for the wisdom to guide them toward a common purpose.

The fate of Thera hung in the balance, and the council's unity would be the key to navigating the perilous path ahead.

Callista rose from her seat, her robes rustling softly as she moved to stand between Theron and Dorian. Her voice, though gentle, carried a quiet authority that commanded the attention of all present. "My friends, let us not forget the reason we have gathered here today. The tremors that shake our island are a reminder that we face a threat far greater than any rivalry or disagreement."

She turned to face each man in turn, her green eyes filled with a compassionate understanding. "Theron, your dedication to the gods and the sacred mysteries is an inspiration to us all. The ancient texts you found regarding our great island have proven invaluable, and we thank you. And Dorian, your knowledge of the wider world and your commitment to reason are equally valuable. But it is only by working together, by combining our strengths and perspectives, that we can hope to save our people."

As Callista spoke, the tension in the room began to dissipate. Theron and Dorian exchanged glances, silently acknowledging the truth in her words. Slowly, almost imperceptibly, they each nodded, their postures relaxing as they turned their attention back to the high priestess.

Ariadne, who had been watching the exchange with wide eyes, leaned forward eagerly. "High Priestess, if I may, again?" she began, her voice bright with enthusiasm. "Perhaps we could involve more community members in our evacuation planning. The fishermen and farmers, the craftsmen and merchants—they all have valuable skills and knowledge that could help us prepare."

Callista smiled warmly at the young priestess, nodding in approval. "An excellent suggestion, Ariadne. The people of Thera are the heart and soul of our island, and their participation will be essential in ensuring a successful evacuation. I think that is a task you would excel at. Captain Minoas will help you in any way he can I am sure." The Captain nodded to Callista in agreement.

As the council members began to discuss Ariadne's idea, the atmosphere in the room shifted. The earlier friction gave way to a sense of shared purpose, as each person contributed their own unique insights and perspectives. Callista watched with quiet satisfaction, knowing that, despite their differences, the council was united in their determination to save their beloved island and its people.

Even as hope bloomed in her heart, Callista could not shake the sense of foreboding that lingered at the edges of her thoughts. The tremors were growing more substantial and more frequent, and she knew that time was running out. They would need to act quickly and decisively if they were to have any chance of success. She closed her eyes momentarily, silently praying to the gods for strength and guidance in the trials to come.

Minoas leaned forward, his weathered hands resting on the stone table. "I agree with young Ariadne," he said, his deep voice resonating through the chamber. "Involving the community is key. But we must also ensure they are prepared for what lies ahead." He paused, his gaze sweeping over the council members. "I propose a series of announcements to familiarize the people with evacuation procedures. We can work with the fishermen to establish safe routes and gather supplies, while the farmers and craftsmen can help fortify our ships with provisions."

Nods of approval rippled through the room as Minoas spoke, his practical approach and authoritative tone lending weight to his words. Callista felt a surge of gratitude for the seasoned captain's presence on the council, knowing that his experience and wisdom would be invaluable in the days to come.

Dorian, his eyes sparkling with inspiration, leaned in to address the council. "Minoas' proposal is excellent, but we must also consider the many facets of this endeavor. Perhaps we could form smaller working groups, each tasked with a specific aspect of the evacuation plan." He smiled, his charm radiating through the room. "By dividing our efforts and collaborating closely, we can ensure that no detail is overlooked and that we are all working in harmony towards our common goal."

As Dorian spoke, Callista could see the lingering tension in the room dissipate, replaced by a growing sense of unity and purpose. His diplomatic approach and adaptable nature were invaluable assets, helping to bridge the gaps between the diverse personalities and backgrounds of the council members.

Callista's heart swelled with pride as she watched her fellow council members rise to the challenge before them. In the face of an unprecedented crisis, they had come together, setting aside their differences and working as one to save their beloved island and its people. She knew that the road ahead would be fraught with challenges and uncertainties, but with the collective strength and wisdom of the council, she believed that they could overcome anything.

Theron, who had been observing the council's interactions with a keen eye, seized the moment to offer his unique perspective. "If I may," he began, his voice steady and assured, "my studies of the mountain have given me insights into the patterns of its tremors. By combining this knowledge with the wisdom of our ancient texts, I believe I can help predict if, and when, a future cataclysm with greater accuracy."

Callista turned her attention to the young priest, her curiosity piqued. "Please, Brother Theron, share your thoughts with us."

Theron nodded, his ink-stained fingers rifling through a stack of parchment filled with meticulous notes and diagrams. "Our traditional interpretations of the mountain's signs have served us well for generations, but I have begun to question whether they fully capture the complexity of the phenomena we are witnessing." He paused, gauging the reactions of his fellow council members before continuing. "By applying a more analytical approach and comparing our records with the actual events, I believe I can refine my prediction and better prepare our people for what lies ahead."

As Theron spoke, Callista could see the council members leaning in, their initial skepticism giving way to genuine interest. His willingness to challenge long-held beliefs and offer fresh perspectives was a testament to his dedication and the depth of his understanding.

She silently thanked the gods for bringing such diverse and talented individuals together in this critical moment. With their combined expertise and unwavering commitment to Thera's well-being, she felt a renewed sense of hope blossoming within her.

However, a nagging concern lingered in the back of Callista's mind. "What of the King?" she asked, her brow furrowed. "He continues to insist that there is no real danger, and I fear his loyal followers may sway the people to remain on the island and make futile sacrifices to the mountain."

A murmur of unease rippled through the council, as each member grappled with the implications of the King's stance. They knew that without the support of the monarch and his cultists, their efforts to ensure the safety of Thera's inhabitants would be greatly hindered.

Theron leaned forward, his eyes narrowed in thought. "The King's influence over his followers is undeniable, but they are small in number, his popularity with the rest of the population is incredibly low." He said, his voice slow and measured. "If we are to ensure the safety of our people, we may need to consider... unconventional methods."

Dorian's eyebrows rose, a flicker of surprise crossing his face. "What exactly are you suggesting, Theron?"

The young priest paused, his gaze locking with Dorian's. "We may need to remove the King's power by... eliminating his most ardent supporters."

A collective gasp echoed through the chamber, as the council members recoiled at the implication of Theron's words. Callista's eyes widened, her heart pounding in her chest as she grappled with the gravity of the suggestion.

To her surprise, Dorian nodded slowly, his expression grave. "As much as it pains me to admit it, Theron may be right," he said, his voice heavy with the weight of the decision. "If the King's cultists continue to sway the people against evacuation, countless lives could be lost."

The council erupted into a heated debate, voices rising and falling as each member grappled with the moral implications of such a drastic action. Callista listened intently, her mind racing as she weighed the potential consequences against the urgent need to protect her people.

As the discussion began to wind down, Callista rose to her feet, her presence commanding the attention of the room. "We will continue to explore all options," she said, her voice steady and resolute. "But let us remember that our ultimate goal is to save lives, not to take them unnecessarily. We must proceed with caution and wisdom, even in the face of great adversity. We cannot act rashly, or in a way that would divide our people. Violence will not help us at this stage."

With that, the council began to disperse, each member lost in their own thoughts as they contemplated the difficult road ahead. Callista, Dorian, and Theron lingered behind, their eyes meeting in a moment of quiet understanding.

Dorian reached for a decanter of wine, pouring three cups and handing them to his companions. "To Thera," he said, raising his cup in a solemn toast. "May we find the strength and unity to guide her through this trial." Callista and Theron echoed the sentiment, their cups clinking softly in the stillness of the chamber. As they sipped the rich, dark liquid, a faint tremor shook the temple, the ground beneath their feet vibrating with an ominous energy.

Chapter 7: The Sacred Cave

The flickering torchlight cast playful shadows across Callista's face as she approached the concealed entrance of the cave. Her dark hair, a cascade of silky strands, swayed gently with each purposeful step she took. The gravel underfoot crunched rhythmically, the solitary sound breaking the reverent silence that enveloped the atmosphere. The air was thick with anticipation, and the subtle scent of earth and moss lingered, enhancing the mystique of the hidden passageway.

"These caves are old and sacred. None from my order have ever brought outsiders here before." She said as she stopped and faced Dorian and Theron. "But I think, if you're to help me and the people of Thera, you need to see what is inside." Theron and Dorian nodded in understanding.

"Stay close," Callista said softly, turning back to the cave entrance. Glancing back at Dorian and Theron to make sure they had heard. "The path can be treacherous if you don't know where to step." She gestured for them to follow, her slender fingers casting long shadows against the rocky walls.

Dorian flashed a reassuring grin. "Don't worry, we'll be right behind you. I'm not about to let a few loose stones get the better of me." His voice held a hint of playful bravado, but his eyes remained fixed on Callista's lithe form, ready to catch her if she stumbled.

Theron merely nodded, his gaze already roaming the cave entrance, drinking in every detail. His mind whirred with possibilities, piecing together fragments of lore and whispered secrets. What mysteries lay hidden within these ancient depths?

As they crossed the threshold, the outside world seemed to fall away, replaced by a cool, earthy dampness that enveloped them like a shroud. Water dripped from unseen heights, each droplet echoing through the shadowed chambers ahead.

Callista paused, her eyes drifting closed as she drew in a slow, centering breath. Her lips moved in a silent prayer, an invocation to Potnia, the Great Mother who held sway over earth, sea, and sky. The gentle murmur of her voice mingled with the cave's primordial song, an ancient harmony that stirred something deep within their souls.

In that moment, Dorian felt a profound sense of awe wash over him. Here, in this place of power, Callista seemed to radiate an otherworldly grace, a connection to the divine that transcended mortal understanding. He glanced at Theron, wondering if the young naturalist felt it too - that humbling realization of just how small they were in the grand tapestry of creation.

Theron met his gaze, a flicker of understanding passing between them. For all his scholarly knowledge, even he could not deny the weight of spiritual presence that permeated the very air they breathed. It was as if the cave itself was alive, whispering secrets of the ages to those who knew how to listen. As they ventured deeper into the cave, their torches cast dancing shadows on the rough-hewn walls, revealing a hidden world of ancient wonders. Theron lifted his torch higher, his eyes widening as the flickering light illuminated a series of intricate frescoes sprawling across the rock face.

"By the gods," he breathed, his voice hushed with reverence. "Callista, look at this."

The High Priestess stepped forward, her gaze sweeping over the vibrant images. Scenes of mountains erupting, people fleeing, then returning. Other frescoes showed people building ships, temples, and bridges. Still others showed people harvesting olives, pressing olives into oil, making wine. But the exploding mountain kept Dorian's gaze the longest.

Dorian leaned in closer, his brow furrowed in curiosity. "What do they depict, exactly?"

Callista traced her fingers along the edge of a particular fresco, her touch gentle and almost reverent. "These are the stories of our people,

Dorian. The trials we have faced, and the guidance of Potnia that has seen us through."

She pointed to a vivid scene of figures fleeing from a mountain spewing fire and ash. "Here, you can see the great eruption that shaped our island, and how our ancestors found safety in the arms of the Mother."

Theron, his analytical mind already whirring, moved closer to examine the frescoes in detail. "The pigments used are remarkable," he mused, his voice filled with wonder. "Such vibrant hues, preserved for centuries in the depths of this cave."

Callista smiled, a flicker of pride in her eyes. "The artisans of Thera are blessed by Potnia herself. Their works are a testament to her glory and the resilience of our people."

Dorian chuckled softly, his gaze drifting from one fresco to the next. "I've seen many wonders in my travels, but nothing quite like this. It's as if the very heart of Thera is laid bare before us."

Theron nodded, his fingers skimming over the intricate details of a scene depicting a procession of worshippers. "The precision of the linework, the depth of the colors... it's extraordinary. These frescoes are more than just art; they're a window into our history, our very identity as Therans."

As they stood there, engrossed in the ancient stories etched upon the walls, a sense of connection washed over them. In that moment, they were more than just individuals - they were part of a tapestry woven across generations, each thread a tale of hope, resilience, and unwavering faith in the face of an ever-changing world.

A sudden, violent tremor shook the cave, sending loose stones clattering to the ground around them. Callista gasped, her hand instinctively reaching out to grasp Dorian's arm as she steadied herself against the wall. "By the Mother,!" she breathed, her eyes wide with alarm.

Theron, his face pale in the flickering torchlight, moved closer to his companions. "An earthquake," he murmured, his voice tight with concern. "We must be cautious. These caves, though sacred, will probably still be treacherous in times of upheaval."

Dorian nodded, his brow furrowed as he glanced toward the entrance. "We should move quickly, but carefully. If the tremors continue, we risk being trapped here."

As if on cue, another shudder rippled through the earth, sending a shower of dust and small rocks cascading from the cave's ceiling. Callista's grip tightened on Dorian's arm, her heart pounding in her chest. She took a deep breath, calling upon the strength of Potnia to steady her nerves, but the passage behind them became blocked with large stones nonetheless.

"Stay close," she urged, her voice ringing with quiet authority. "We'll navigate these passages together, with the Mother's guidance. She will not abandon us in our time of need."

Theron and Dorian exchanged a glance, then both glanced at the path they'd followed into the cave, now rendered impassable. Their expressions a mix of anxiety and fear. They fell into step behind Callista, their torches held high to illuminate the path ahead.

As they pressed deeper into the cave, the air grew thick with dust, the sounds of their footsteps and labored breathing echoing off the narrow walls. Callista's mind raced, her thoughts torn between the need to find a way out and the gnawing fear that their sacred sanctuary might crumble around them.

"There," Dorian called out, pointing to a small opening in the rock face. "That passage might lead us to another chamber, perhaps even an alternate exit."

Callista squinted, trying to peer through the swirling dust. The opening was narrow, barely wide enough for a person to squeeze through, but it was their best chance. She nodded, steeling herself for the challenge ahead. She knew these caves, but some rock had clearly shifted from the tremors since the last time she had been here.

"We'll have to go one at a time," she said, her voice strained but resolute. "I'll go first, then Theron, and Dorian, you bring up the rear. If anything happens, if the cave starts to collapse..."

She trailed off, unable to give voice to the unthinkable. Dorian reached out, his hand resting gently on her shoulder. "We'll make it through this, together," he assured her, his eyes shining with a mix of concern and encouragement. "The Mother's strength flows through us all."

With a final, shared look of determination, Callista turned to face the narrow passage. She took a deep breath, whispered a prayer to Potnia, and began to crawl through the opening, the cool stone pressing against her skin as she inched her way forward into the unknown depths of the cave.

As Callista emerged from the narrow passage, her eyes widened in wonder. The chamber before her glittered with an ethereal light, casting a soft glow on the ancient rock formations. The countless crystals, seemed to glow from some source of light behind them, or inside them. They adorned the walls and ceiling, transforming the cave into a mesmerizing sanctuary. Despite coming to these sacred caves many times before, this chamber had never glowed the way it was now. As if something behind its walls, ceiling, and floor, had awakened and cast brilliant light, and warmth through the subterranean dreamscape.

"By the Mother's grace," Theron whispered as he crawled out behind her, his voice tinged with awe. "I've never seen anything like this."

Dorian, bringing up the rear, let out a low whistle of appreciation. "It's as if the stars themselves have descended into the heart of the earth," he marveled, his eyes dancing with wonder.

“In all my times here, this cavern was cold, and dark. The crystals smooth, but lifeless. Now though... the crystalline columns and walls glow brightly in beautiful hues of greens, blues, purple, and indigo." Callista said to them.

Theron reached out and touched one of the massive crystal pillars. "They're so warm. I didn't know this could happen."

"They radiate such a soft light too, not bright, not dim... it's soft like down feathers." Dorian's expression crinkled in contemplation.

For a moment, the trio stood in silence, their fears momentarily forgotten as they absorbed the breathtaking beauty surrounding them. The crystals seemed to pulse with a gentle rhythm, almost as if the cave itself were alive, breathing in sync with the island above.

Callista felt a wave of peace wash over her, the divine presence of Potnia palpable in the air. She closed her eyes, offering a silent prayer of gratitude for this moment of respite amidst the chaos.

"We should rest here, if only for a short while," she suggested, her voice soft and reverent. "Regain our strength before we continue on."

Theron nodded, already reaching for his satchel to retrieve his water skin. "Agreed. We'll need to be alert and focused when we start moving again."

As they settled into the crystal chamber, Callista couldn't help but feel a glimmer of hope reigniting within her. Perhaps this was a sign from the Mother, a reminder that even in the darkest of times, beauty and light could still be found. With renewed determination, she began to plan their next steps, her mind already reaching out to the wisdom of Potnia for guidance.

Callista, Dorian, and Theron huddled together in the crystal chamber, their faces illuminated by the soft, ethereal glow. As they caught their breath, the weight of their shared experience settled upon them, forging an unspoken bond that transcended their differences.

Dorian was the first to break the silence. "I never thought I'd find myself in a situation like this," he admitted, a wry smile tugging at his lips. "But there's no one I'd rather be trapped with than you two."

Callista chuckled softly, her green eyes sparkling in the crystal light. "I couldn't agree more, Dorian. The Mother works in mysterious ways, bringing us together when we need each other most."

Theron nodded, his gaze thoughtful as he looked around the chamber. "It's strange, isn't it? How adversity can create such strong connections between people."

"It's a testament to the resilience of our Theran spirit," Callista mused, her voice warm with admiration. "In times of crisis, we find strength in one another, in the bonds we forge through shared hardship."

"Theran, and one Cypriate's, spirit." Dorian corrected a playful glint in his eye, and the three companions laughed, filling the crystalline chamber with a beautiful, resonant sound.

As they sat in companionable silence, their thoughts turned to the future of Thera. Theron was the first to voice his concerns, his brow furrowed with worry.

"What if we can't stop the eruption? What if we can't get everyone off the island? What if the frescoes are wrong, and this time the islands don't grow in size, it explodes like the mountains Dorian and the Captain described seeing on their voyages?" he asked, his voice barely above a whisper. "What will become of our people, our sacred island?"

Dorian reached out, placing a comforting hand on Theron's shoulder. "We can't lose hope, my friend. We've already come this far, and we'll continue to fight for Thera with every breath we take."

Callista nodded, her eyes shining with determination. "Dorian is right. We must have faith in ourselves and in the wisdom of Potnia. She would not have brought us together if she didn't believe we could make a difference. Even if that means starting ove somewhere else."

With renewed determination, Callista stood to lead the way through the narrowing passages, her torch casting dancing shadows on the cave walls. Dorian followed close behind, his eyes scanning the rocky terrain for potential hazards, while Theron brought up the rear, his keen observations guiding their steps.

"Watch your footing here," Callista warned, gesturing to a cluster of loose stones. "The path is becoming more treacherous." Dorian nodded, carefully navigating the obstacle. "We'll need to be cautious. Caves like these can be unpredictable."

As they pressed on, a steep incline required them to work together, forming a human chain to ascend the slippery slope. Callista's leadership shone through as she directed their efforts, her calm demeanor a steadying influence.

"Just a little further," she encouraged, her voice echoing in the confined space. "We can do this."

Theron, his analytical mind always at work, spotted a narrow crevice that seemed to offer an alternative route. "Over here," he called out, pointing to the opening. "This might lead us around the obstruction."

Dorian, ever adaptable, squeezed through the tight space first, his broad shoulders barely fitting. "It's a bit of a tight squeeze," he chuckled, "but it looks like it opens up ahead."

As they emerged from the crevice, Callista couldn't help but marvel at the way her companions' unique strengths complemented each other. Dorian's adaptability and Theron's keen observations had proven invaluable, while her own leadership had kept them focused on their goal.

Finally, after what felt like an eternity, they spotted a glimmer of light ahead. "Look!" Theron exclaimed, his voice filled with hope. "I think that's a way out."

Callista's heart pounded with anticipation as she approached the narrow opening, the sunlight streaming in like a beacon of hope. She stepped through first, blinking as her eyes adjusted to the sudden brightness.

Dorian and Theron followed close behind, their faces breaking into relieved smiles as they emerged into the open air. The trio stood for a moment, savoring the feeling of the sun on their skin and the fresh breeze in their hair.

"We made it," Callista breathed, her voice filled with a mix of exhaustion and triumph. "Together."

Callista took a deep breath, the salty sea air filling her lungs as she surveyed the familiar landscape before her. The island of Thera stretched out like a tapestry, its vibrant colors and textures woven together by the hand of the Mother Goddess herself. Yet even amidst the beauty, an undercurrent of unease tugged at her heart.

"The journey through the cave has shown us that we must be prepared for the challenges ahead," she said softly, her gaze distant. "The tremors, the omens... Potnia is trying to tell us something."

Dorian placed a comforting hand on her shoulder. "Whatever lies ahead, we'll face it together. The people of Thera are resilient, and with your guidance, we'll weather any storm." Theron nodded in agreement, his brow furrowed in thought.

"The cave paintings depicted past eruptions and evacuations. Perhaps they hold clues to what we must do now." Theron said.

Callista turned to her companions, a flicker of determination in her eyes. "You're right. The answers we seek may lie in the wisdom of our ancestors. We must study our people's past more closely."

Chapter 8: Flames of Desire

Callista's hand tingled as Dorian's warm fingers interlaced with hers. The swell of music beckoned them onto the packed dance floor, couples twirling and weaving around them. As they stepped forward, it felt like the most natural thing in the world.

Callista met Dorian's hazel eyes, alight with the flickering glow of paper lanterns strung overhead. A small smile played at his lips. "Shall we?"

She squeezed his hand in response. "Let's dance."

As if they had rehearsed it, their bodies moved in perfect harmony, feet gliding across the stone floor in time to the jaunty melody. Dorian's hand rested at the small of her back, guiding her through the steps. Callista marveled at how in sync they were, anticipating each other's movements by instinct alone.

All around them, the harvest festival was in full swing. The mouthwatering aroma of sizzling meats and honey-soaked pastries mingled with woodsmoke on the evening breeze. Villagers clapped and cheered as the dancers whirled past in a kaleidoscope of colorful robes. Underfoot, Callista could feel the pulsing rhythms reverberating through the ground, as if the very earth was dancing with them.

Her thoughts scattered as Dorian spun her out gracefully, then drew her back into his arms. She gasped, breathless with exhilaration and something more. The way his eyes never left her face, the heat of his palm through the thin fabric at her waist - it felt intimate, exhilarating...dangerous.

"You're quite light on your feet, High Priestess," Dorian murmured, his breath warm against her ear. "I wouldn't have guessed."

"You're not so bad yourself," she quipped. "For a salty seafarer."

His chest rumbled with a low chuckle. They spun agai, and Callista caught glimpses of other dancers watching them, admiring whispers floating by. Let them look, she thought giddily. Tonight, under the twinkling stars, she was more than just a priestess. She was a woman, alive and alight with possibility.

As the final notes faded, Dorian dipped her low, his face inches from hers. Callista's heart raced. Around them, the crowd erupted into applause, but she scarcely heard it over the roaring of her pulse. Slowly, Dorian drew her upright, his hands lingering at her waist a moment longer than was strictly necessary. She knew people must be watching, but she couldn't bring herself to care. Not when he was looking at her like that.

"Thank you for the dance, Callista," he said softly, reluctantly letting her go.

She instantly missed his touch. "The pleasure was all mine."

***

Theron stood at the edge of the dance floor, his heart pounding in time with the music, though not from exertion. His eyes remained fixed on Callista and Dorian as they moved together, their bodies in perfect sync, as if they'd been dancing together for years. The way Dorian's hand rested on the small of Callista's back, the way she leaned into him as they spun, the brilliant smile on her face - it all made Theron's chest tighten with an unfamiliar ache.

He'd always admired Callista, respected her as a leader and a fellow theologian. But seeing her like this, radiant and carefree in Dorian's arms, stirred something deeper within him. And Dorian... Theron's gaze lingered on the sailor's broad shoulders, the confident grace of his movements. He looked away quickly, his face heating.

What was wrong with him? He shouldn't be feeling this way, not about either of them. It was wrong, inappropriate. And yet, he couldn't seem to stop his heart from yearning.

As the dance ended, Callista and Dorian shared a long look, their faces mere inches apart. Theron's breath caught in his throat. For a moment, he thought they might kiss, right there in front of everyone. But then they stepped apart, fingers brushing as they separated.

Theron watched as they wove through the crowd, Dorian's hand hovering near the small of Callista's back, their bodies still attuned to each other. They were heading in his direction, he realized with a jolt of panic. What would he say? How could he possibly hide the turmoil inside him?

But then Callista spotted him and her face lit up. "Theron! There you are!" She reached out and grasped his hand, pulling him into a quick embrace. He stiffened, keenly aware of Dorian's eyes on them.

"We were just coming to find you," Dorian said, clapping him on the shoulder. His touch burned through Theron's robes. "Thought you might like to join us for a drink."

"I..." Theron's mouth went dry. He glanced between them, at their flushed faces and bright eyes. They looked so happy, so right together. Who was he to intrude on that? "I appreciate the offer, but I should probably turn in for the night. Early morning prayers, you know."

Callista's smile faltered. "Are you sure? It's still early..."

"I'm sure," he said, mustering a strained smile. "You two enjoy yourselves. I'll see you in the morning." He bowed his head to Callista, nodded at Dorian, and then hurried away before they could protest further.

As he wove through the crowd, his heart raced and his mind whirled. What was happening to him? These feelings, they went against all he had learned, all he held true. Still, he couldn't refute their power.

He glanced back once, just in time to see Callista lean close to whisper something in Dorian's ear. Dorian laughed, his head thrown back, then tucked a stray lock of hair behind Callista's ear with a tenderness that made Theron's chest ache.

Tearing his gaze away, Theron hurried into the night, praying to Potnia for guidance. But deep down, he feared that even the Mother

Goddess herself might not have answers for the forbidden desires taking root in his heart.

***

The silvery moonlight filtered through the gnarled branches of the ancient olive trees, casting dappled shadows across Callista and Dorian's faces as they wandered hand-in-hand into the secluded grove. The distant sounds of music and laughter from the harvest festival faded, replaced by the gentle whisper of leaves rustling in the balmy night breeze.

Callista's heart raced, her skin tingling where Dorian's fingers intertwined with hers. She couldn't remember the last time she'd felt so alive, so free. With Dorian, she could simply be Callista, not the High Priestess weighted down by duty and tradition.

"It's beautiful here," Dorian murmured, his voice low and intimate. "Almost as beautiful as you."

A flush crept up Callista's neck. "Flatterer," she accused, but a smile tugged at her lips.

Dorian grinned, unrepentant. "It's not flattery if it's true."

"A very base form of flattery at that. I nearly cringed in embarassment for you." Callista teased and Dorian laughed a loud, unbridled laugh.

He tugged her closer, and Callista went willingly, drawn to his warmth, his vitality. Out here, away from prying eyes, she could let herself imagine, just for a moment, what it might be like to choose her own path, to follow her heart instead of the dictates of her station.

Dorian's free hand came up to cup her cheek, his callused thumb brushing feather-light over her skin. Callista's breath caught. In his eyes, she saw the same longing, the same aching need that consumed her.

"Callista," he breathed, her name a prayer on his lips. "Tell me you feel this too. This connection between us."

"I do," she whispered, her voice trembling. "Gods help me, but I do."

And then his mouth was on hers, and the world fell away. His lips, soft yet insistent, moved against hers with a passion that stole her breath. She melted into him, her hands fisting in the fabric of his tunic, anchoring herself to him as desire, hot and urgent, unfurled within her.

Dorian's arms encircled her, pulling her flush against the hard planes of his body. A soft moan escaped her as his tongue traced the seam of her lips, seeking entrance. She opened for him, the kiss turning deep and drugging, a heady mix of wine and spice and something uniquely Dorian.

In that moment, nothing existed but the two of them, lost in a tangle of lips and tongues and shared breaths. The future, with all its uncertainties and obstacles, seemed far away, a distant concern compared to the bliss of being in Dorian's arms.

But even as she surrendered to the kiss, to the glorious sensations he evoked in her, a tiny voice in the back of Callista's mind whispered a warning. She was playing with fire, risking everything for a forbidden taste of freedom.

And yet, as Dorian's lips trailed from her mouth to her jaw, his beard rasping deliciously against her sensitive skin, Callista couldn't bring herself to care. For this one stolen moment, she would let herself have what she wanted, consequences be damned.

The goddess would forgive her this one transgression. And if not, well... Callista would pay that price willingly for the chance to know, just once, what it felt like to truly live.

A twig snapped behind them, the sound as loud as a thunderclap in the quiet grove. Callista and Dorian sprang apart, spinning to face the intruder with hearts racing and breath coming in short, sharp bursts.

Theron stood frozen at the edge of the clearing, his face a mask of shock and confusion. "Callista? Dorian? What... what's going on here?"

Callista swallowed hard, her mind scrambling for an explanation, an excuse, anything to defuse the tension crackling in the air. But before she could speak, Dorian stepped forward, his voice steady despite the emotions swirling in his eyes.

"Theron, I know this must come as a surprise, but please, hear us out."

Theron's gaze darted between them, his brow furrowed as he tried to make sense of the scene before him. "I don't understand. You two... you're not... this isn't right."

Callista's heart clenched at the hurt and betrayal in Theron's voice. She moved to stand beside Dorian, her hand finding his and twining their fingers together in a silent show of unity.

"Theron, I know this is complicated, and I'm sorry you had to find out like this. But what's happening between Dorian and me... it's real. It's true."

Theron shook his head, his eyes glistening with unshed tears. "But what about your duties, Callista? Your sacred vows? And Dorian, you're a sailor, you will one day move on from Thera." The implications of what Theron said hung thick in the night air between them like a fog bank suddenly rolling in.

Dorian sighed, his shoulders slumping under the weight of Theron's accusations. "It's not that simple, Theron. We didn't plan for this to happen, but sometimes the heart wants what it wants, no matter how much we try to deny it."

Callista nodded, her voice soft but firm. "I know it goes against everything we've been taught, Theron, but I can't ignore what I feel for Dorian. It's like the goddess herself has blessed our union, even if it defies the laws of man."

Theron looked away, his jaw clenching as he struggled to process their words. "I don't know what to say. I never thought... I mean, I always assumed..." He trailed off, his voice breaking on a choked sob.

Callista's heart ached for him, for the pain and confusion he must be feeling. She released Dorian's hand and stepped forward, reaching out to touch Theron's arm in a gesture of comfort.

"Theron, please, talk to us. Tell us what you're thinking, what you're feeling. We want to understand, to find a way through this together."

Theron met her gaze, his eyes swimming with a tumult of emotions. "I...I don't know, Callista. I need time to think, to wrap my head around all of this. It's just...it's a lot to take in."

Dorian nodded, his expression sympathetic. "We understand, Theron. Take all the time you need. But know that we're here for you, no matter what. You're not alone in this."

Theron stood for a moment staring at the sky, his voice wavering with a mix of vulnerability and hope. "I can't deny that I feel drawn to both of you. It is as if the gods have woven our paths together for a reason Callista." He paused, his gaze shifting between Callista and Dorian, seeking understanding in their eyes. "Perhaps we could explore these feelings together, see where they lead us. I know it's unconventional, but nothing about our situation has been ordinary."

Dorian listened intently, his brow furrowed in contemplation. The soft rustle of olive leaves in the breeze filled the momentary silence as he gathered his thoughts. Finally, he spoke, his voice steady despite the whirlwind of emotions within. "I'd be lying if I said I hadn't felt the same pull towards you both. It's as if the very air between us is charged with possibility."

He took a step closer, his hand reaching out to brush against Callista's, their fingers intertwining as naturally as breathing. "I've never been with a man before," he admitted, his gaze locking with Theron's, "but I'm willing to open my heart to the idea, to see where this path may lead us."

Callista felt a warmth bloom in her chest, a sense of rightness settling over her like a comforting blanket. She squeezed Dorian's hand, offering a reassuring smile before turning to Theron. "The gods work in mysterious ways, but I believe they've brought us together for a reason. Let us honor their plan and explore this connection between us, with open hearts and minds."

Theron's shoulders visibly relaxed, relief and gratitude softening his features. "Thank you, both of you, for being willing to embrace this. I know it won't be easy, but I have faith that together, we can weather any storm."

As if on cue, a gentle breeze picked up, carrying with it the distant sounds of the festival, a reminder of the world beyond their secluded haven. Callista breathed deeply, the scent of olives and earth grounding her in the moment. "Come," she said, her voice warm with affection, "let us return to the celebration, united in purpose and in heart."

Hand in hand, the trio emerged from the grove, their footsteps falling into sync as they made their way back to the vibrant lights and joyous sounds of the harvest festival. Though the path ahead was uncertain, one thing was clear: they would face it together, bound by a love that defied convention and a shared destiny that called them ever onward.

As they walked, a distant rumble echoed through the night, barely audible over the sounds of the festival. Callista paused, her brow furrowing as she strained to listen. The ground trembled slightly beneath their feet, a subtle vibration that sent a shiver down her spine.

Dorian's grip on her hand tightened, his eyes scanning the horizon. "Did you feel that?" he asked, his voice low and cautious.

Theron nodded, his gaze fixed on the distant peak of the volcano. "The mountain stirs," he murmured, a hint of unease creeping into his tone. "It's a reminder that even as we celebrate, the gods hold the power to reshape our world in an instant."

Callista's heart raced, the weight of her responsibilities as High Priestess pressing down upon her. She knew that the fate of her people was inextricably linked to the moods of the earth and the whims of the gods. The volcano's rumble was a stark reminder of the precarious balance that sustained their way of life.

"We must be vigilant," she said, her voice steady despite the unease that coiled within her. "The gods have granted us this moment of joy, but we cannot forget the duties that lie ahead."

Dorian's thumb traced a soothing circle on the back of her hand, his touch a silent promise of support. "Together, we'll face whatever challenges the gods see fit to send our way."

Theron's gaze softened as he looked at them, a flicker of hope amid the uncertainty. "With the strength of our bond and the guidance of the gods, I believe we can weather any storm."

As they resumed their walk, the distant rumble faded, swallowed by the sounds of laughter and music that spilled from the festival grounds. Yet the memory of the tremor lingered. Callista's heart swelled with a fierce determination tempered by the warmth of the two men at her side. Together, they would navigate the complexities of their newfound connection, even as they worked to unravel the mysteries that threatened their sacred isle.

Chapter 9: The Priest King's Decree

The heavy wooden doors groaned as Callista pushed them open, her crimson robes billowing behind her like the unfurling petals of a rose. She strode into the council chamber, her sandaled feet echoing against the polished stone floor. The room fell silent, save for the hushed murmurs of anticipation that rippled through the gathered council members. They sat around the large stone table, carved with intricate symbols of the goddess Potnia, their expressions a mottled canvas of curiosity and skepticism.

Callista's heart thrummed in her chest as she took her place at the center of the chamber, the scent of frankincense tickling her nostrils. She met the gazes of the council members, offering a serene smile despite the tension that crackled in the air like a gathering storm.

As she prepared to speak, Priest King Lykos rose from his seat at the head of the table, his ornate robes of deep blue and gold glinting in the flickering torchlight. He cleared his throat, the sound cutting through the murmurs like a knife through silk.

"Esteemed members of the council," Lykos began, his voice smooth as honey yet laced with an underlying edge. "We gather here today to address a matter of great importance to our sacred island."

He paused, his steely gray eyes scanning the faces of those assembled. "In light of recent events, and after much contemplation, I have reached a decision. A decree, if you will, to ensure the continued order and stability of our community."

Callista tilted her head slightly, studying Lykos' expression. The set of his jaw and the glint in his eye hinted at something more than mere caution. She braced herself, knowing that whatever decree he was about to announce would likely challenge her own standing and the traditions she held dear.

Lykos continued, his voice rising with each word. "From this day forth, all temple activities will be restricted and subject to the approval of the Priest King. We cannot allow the delicate balance of our society to be disrupted by unverified claims or misguided interpretations of the goddess' will."

The chamber erupted in a cacophony of gasps and murmurs, council members turning to one another with wide eyes and furrowed brows. Callista remained still, her expression a mask of calm determination, even as a flicker of disbelief danced in her emerald eyes.

She drew in a deep breath, the scent of incense mingling with the tang of tension that hung heavy in the air. As the council's gazes turned to her, Callista silently prayed to Potnia for the strength and wisdom to navigate the challenges that lay ahead. She knew that this decree was but the first move in a complex dance of power and faith, and she was determined to lead her people through the storm with unwavering grace and conviction.

As the murmurs died down, Callista stepped forward, her voice steady and clear. "Esteemed council members, I understand the need for caution in these uncertain times. However, I must respectfully disagree with this decree. The omens I have interpreted carry a sense of urgency that cannot be ignored."

She paused, her eyes scanning the faces of the council members. "The signs from the goddess are clear. We must act swiftly to prepare for the challenges that lie ahead. Restricting temple activities will only hinder our ability to seek guidance and protect our people."

Lykos countered with a dismissive wave of his hand. "High Priestess Callista, while we value your dedication to the goddess, we must also consider the possibility that your judgment may be clouded."

His eyes narrowed, a hint of a smirk playing at the corners of his mouth. "Your association with the outsider, Dorian, has not gone unnoticed. Perhaps his presence has influenced your interpretations, leading you astray from the true path. Perhaps he has other motives for wanting Thera to be in a weakened state. Perhaps the Cypriate fleet waits, just over the horizon," Lykos motions out the window to the sea dramatically, "waiting for us to evacuate our home so they can sail in and take all that we've built over the centuries."

Callista's heart raced at the mention of Dorian, but she maintained her composure. "My association with Dorian has no bearing on my ability to interpret the sacred mysteries. The omens speak for themselves, and it is my duty to convey their message to the council and the people of Thera."

Lykos' words hung in the air, casting a shadow of doubt over the assembly. Council members exchanged glances, their expressions a mix of uncertainty and speculation.

Callista's mind raced as she searched for the right words to sway the council. She knew that Lykos' accusation was a calculated move to undermine her credibility and maintain his own grip on power. She silently vowed to herself that she would not let his machinations stand in the way of protecting her beloved island and its people.

The council chamber was cloaked in tense silence as Callista stood before the assembly, her gaze fixed firmly on Lykos. She could feel the weight of his skepticism bearing down on her, and she knew that she had to act swiftly to dispel his doubts.

With a deep breath, she addressed the assembly once more. "My fellow council members, I understand your reservations about these omens and their implications. But I urge you to consider the gravity of our situation."

She paused as she scanned the faces of the council members, her eyes locking onto each one in turn. "We are facing uncertain times, and it is only through the guidance of Potnia that we can hope to find our way forward."

Lykos' expression remained impassive as Callista continued. "I know that some of you may question my judgment due to my association with Dorian. But let me remind you all that he has proven himself time and time again as a faithful ally to our people."

A murmur rippled through the assembly at this, some nodding in agreement while others looked unsure.

“Furthermore,” Callista continued, her voice growing stronger with each passing word, “my bond with Dorian does not diminish my devotion to our goddess or cloud my ability to interpret her messages.”

She could see Lykos’ expression shifting from smugness to something more akin to anger as she spoke. She knew that he resented Dorian’s influence over her and saw him as a threat to his own power.

But Callista refused to let such petty concerns distract her from her duty. She had been chosen by Potnia for a reason, and she would not back down now.

“You all know me,” she said firmly. “You know of my unwavering commitment to Thera and its people. Do you truly believe that I would put them in harm’s way without good reason?”

The words seemed to strike a chord with some of the council members, and Callista could see the uncertainty in

Dorian stepped forward, his sun-kissed skin seeming to glow in the flickering light of the bronze braziers. "Esteemed council members," he began, his voice carrying the rhythmic cadence of a seasoned storyteller, "I come before you today not as an outsider, but as a witness to the power of nature's fury."

He paused, his warm brown eyes scanning the faces of the assembled council. "In my travels, I have seen firsthand the devastation wrought by earthquakes and volcanic eruptions. I have watched as entire cities were swallowed by the earth, their people left homeless and destitute."

Dorian's words painted a vivid picture, and the council members leaned forward, their attention rapt. "I believe that Callista's interpretations of the omens are not mere fancy, but a warning of what is to come. We must heed her words and take action to protect your people and your sacred island."

Theron, moved to stand next to Dorian, nodding in agreement. "I have spent countless hours observing the earth-signs," he said, his voice quiet but firm. "The increased tremors, the changes in the mountain's smoke, and the restlessness of the animals all point to an impending disaster."

He drew a small notebook from his satchel, flipping through the pages filled with his meticulous observations. "I have recorded the frequency and intensity of these signs, and the pattern is clear. We cannot ignore the evidence before us."

Lykos scoffed, his eyes narrowing. "You would have us trust the word of a foreigner and a young priest from Akrotiri over the wisdom of our traditions?"

Dorian met Lykos' gaze, his expression unwavering. "I speak not as a foreigner, but as a friend to the people of Thera. I have seen the strength and resilience of your people, and I believe that together, we can face any challenge that comes our way. The people of Thera saved my life, and many lives from my doomed ship as it broke upon your islands rocks in the storm. I have a life debt to repay. To all of you."

Theron stepped forward, his voice growing stronger. "And I speak not as a mere priest from small Akrotiri, but as a devoted servant of Potnia. My observations are grounded in both faith and reason, and I believe that it is our sacred duty to act upon them."

As Dorian and Theron spoke, Callista felt a surge of hope. Their words lent credence to her own warnings, and she could see the doubt beginning to fade from the faces of the council members. Perhaps, with their help, she could finally convince the council to take action and prepare for the coming disaster.

The council members exchanged glances, their uncertainty palpable in the flickering light of the braziers. Callista seized the moment, stepping forward with her hands outstretched, the sacred beads on her wrist glinting softly. "Esteemed members of the council,

I implore you to consider the welfare of our community. The signs are clear, and we must act now to protect our people."

Her voice resonated through the chamber, echoing off the ancient stone walls. "As servants of Potnia, it is our sacred duty to heed her warnings and prepare for the worst. We cannot let our people suffer when we have the power to prevent it."

Lykos, sensing his influence waning, rose to his feet, his ceremonial robes rustling with the sudden movement. "And what of tradition?" he demanded, his rigid posture underscoring his determination to preserve the status quo. "For generations, our people have looked to the priest-king for guidance and stability. To abandon our ways now would be to invite chaos and disorder."

He gestured to the elaborate frescoes adorning the walls, depicting the glorious history of Thera. "Our ancestors built this great civilization on the foundation of our sacred traditions. We cannot simply cast them aside at the first sign of trouble."

Callista met his gaze, her green eyes shining with conviction. "But what good are traditions if they do not serve the people? Our ancestors also taught us to adapt and change when necessary, to ensure the survival of our community."

She turned to face the council members, her voice softening. "I know that change can be frightening, but we must have the courage to do what is right for our people. We have faced challenges before, and we have always emerged stronger for it."

As she spoke, Callista could feel the energy in the room shifting, the uncertainty giving way to a sense of purpose. She knew that her words were striking a chord with the council members, reminding them of their duty to protect and serve the people of Thera.

Lykos, however, refused to yield. "And what of the priest-king's authority?" he demanded, his voice growing louder. "Would you have us undermine the very foundation of our society?"

Callista shook her head, her dark hair swaying with the movement. "No, Sire. I would have us work together, as we have always done. The priest-king's authority is not diminished by heeding the wisdom of the priests and priestesses. In fact, it is strengthened by it."

She could see the doubt in Lykos' eyes, the realization that his arguments were losing their power. And yet, she knew that he would not give up easily. He was a man accustomed to wielding power, and he would not relinquish it without a fight.

But Callista was ready for the challenge. She had the support of Dorian and Theron, and the growing conviction of the council members. Together, they would find a way to protect the people of Thera, no matter what obstacles lay ahead.

As the debate intensified, council members began to voice their opinions, some siding with Callista, others with Lykos. The air grew thick with the scent of incense and the sound of raised voices, each person determined to make their case heard.

"The High Priestess speaks the truth!" declared Councilman Demetrios, his deep voice booming through the chamber. "We cannot ignore the signs any longer. We must act now to ensure the safety of our people."

"And risk throwing our island into chaos?" retorted Councilwoman Adrasteia, her sharp eyes narrowing. "We must proceed with caution and maintain order above all else."

Callista listened intently to each argument, her mind working to find the right words to sway the council. She could feel the weight of responsibility pressing down upon her, the knowledge that the fate of Thera rested on the outcome of this debate.

"My friends," she began, her voice calm and measured, "I understand your concerns. Change can be frightening, and the unknown can be daunting. But we cannot let our fear blind us to the truth."

She paused, letting her words sink in before continuing. "The signs are clear. The earth trembles beneath our feet, the sea churns and warms all around our island, the fish are dricen far from our shores, foul smells come from the cracks in the earth. We must heed these warnings and take action, even if it means challenging the way things have always been done."

Lykos scoffed, his face twisted with disdain. "You speak of truth, High Priestess, but what proof do you have? These so-called signs could be nothing more than the ravings of a fevered mind."

Callista met his gaze unflinchingly, her green eyes blazing with conviction. "The proof is all around us, Lykos. In the tremors that shake our homes, in the smells that rise from the earth, from the warming water, in the unease that grips our hearts. We cannot afford to ignore these signs any longer."

She could see the doubt flickering in the eyes of some council members, the uncertainty that came with challenging long-held beliefs. But she could also see the glimmer of hope, the desire to do what was right for the people of Thera.

"I ask you not to blindly follow my words, but to look within yourselves and listen to the wisdom of your own hearts. What does your intuition tell you? What does your love for our people demand of you?"

The chamber fell silent, each council member lost in their own thoughts. Callista could feel the tension in the air, the weight of the decision that lay before them. And then, slowly but surely, the tide began to turn. One by one, council members began to nod their heads, their expressions shifting from doubt to determination.

"The High Priestess is right," said Councilman Nikos, his voice gruff but firm. "We must put the needs of our people first, even if it means challenging tradition."

Lykos looked around the room, his face growing red with anger as he realized he was losing control. "You would all follow this woman blindly? You would risk everything we have built on the word of a mere priestess?" But his words fell on deaf ears. The council had made its decision, and there was no turning back now. Callista felt a rush of relief wash over her, the knowledge that she had succeeded in her mission. But she knew that the real work was only just beginning. They had a long road ahead of them, and many challenges to face.

But for now, she allowed herself a moment of triumph, a moment to savor the victory that had been hard-won. She looked around the room, meeting the eyes of each council member in turn, and saw the same determination and resolve reflected back at her.

Amid the heated debate, Dorian and Theron had exchanged a knowing glance, their eyes conveying a silent message of solidarity. They stood shoulder to shoulder, their presence a beacon of unwavering support for Callista. The scent of incense hung heavy in the air, mingling with the rising tension as voices grew louder and more impassioned.

Callista's gaze flickered towards her companions, drawing strength from their steadfast presence. She took a deep breath, the sacred beads in her hair clinking softly as she prepared to speak once more. But before she could utter a word, the ground beneath their feet began to tremble.

The sudden tremor sent a ripple of fear through the council chamber, the stone walls groaning under the strain. Goblets of wine toppled, their crimson contents spilling across the polished table like blood. The room fell silent, save for the ominous rumble of the earth itself.

Dorian instinctively reached out to steady Theron, his strong hands gripping the younger man's shoulders. "It's happening," he whispered, his voice low and urgent. "Just as we warned."

Theron nodded, his eyes wide with a mix of awe and trepidation. "The signs were there all along," he murmured, his mind racing with the implications of the quake. "We must act now, before it's too late."

As the tremor subsided, leaving an eerie stillness in its wake, all eyes turned to Callista. She stood tall and resolute, her green eyes blazing with a fierce determination. The tremor had served as a powerful reminder of the impending danger, lending an undeniable weight to her warnings. "You see now," she said, her voice clear and unwavering, "the very earth cries out for action. We cannot afford to ignore the signs any longer."

Lykos, his face pale and his hands shaking, struggled to maintain his composure. "Perhaps... perhaps there is wisdom in your words, High Priestess," he conceded, his pride crumbling in the face of the undeniable evidence.

The council members exchanged glances, their expressions a mix of fear and resolve. The time for debate had passed; now was the moment for unity and decisive action. Callista's heart swelled with a fierce pride as she looked upon the faces of her fellow council members. She knew that the path ahead would be fraught with challenges, but with Dorian and Theron by her side, and the support of the council, she was ready to face whatever lay ahead.

The tremor had shaken more than just the chamber; it had shaken the very foundations of their society. And in its wake, a new path had been forged, one that would lead them towards a future of hope and resilience. As the council members began to voice their support, Callista felt a wave of relief wash over her. She had known that convincing them would not be an easy task, but the tremor had provided the catalyst she needed to sway even the most stubborn among them.

Callista felt a surge of gratitude towards Lykos. She knew that it could not have been easy for him to admit that she had been right all along, and she respected him for his willingness to put the needs of the community above his own pride.

As the council members began to discuss the specifics of their plan, Callista caught Dorian's eye from across the room. He gave her a small nod, his eyes shining with pride and admiration. She felt a warmth spread through her chest, knowing that she had his unwavering support.

Theron, too, seemed to sense the shift in the room. He stepped forward, his voice calm and measured. "I suggest we begin by assessing our current resources," he said. "We must know what we have at our disposal before we can effectively plan for the future."

The council members murmured their agreement, and soon the chamber was filled with the sound of productive discussion. Callista felt a sense of hope blossoming within her. They had a long road ahead of them, but with the council united and the wisdom of the earth-signs to guide them, she knew that they would find a way to weather the storm.

As the meeting drew to a close, Callista took a moment to offer a silent prayer to Potnia. She thanked the Great Mother for her guidance and strength, and asked for her continued protection in the days to come.

With a final nod to the council members, Callista turned and strode from the chamber, her robes billowing behind her. She knew that there was much work to be done, but for now, she allowed herself a moment of quiet satisfaction. They had taken the first step towards safeguarding their people, and that was a victory worth celebrating.

Chapter 10: Tremors of the Heart

Callista stood at the temple's entrance, her fingertips pressed against the cool stone columns. The ground trembled beneath her sandaled feet, sending a shiver up her spine. She watched as the sacred flames in the bronze braziers flickered and danced, casting eerie shadows across the temple walls.

Her heart raced as she whispered a prayer. "Great Potnia, guide us through these troubled times. Give me the strength and wisdom to lead our people."

Taking a deep breath, Callista turned and strode briskly through the temple corridors. Her mind swirled with thoughts of the recent omens - the tremors, the restless livestock, the strange behavior of birds and fish. As she walked, Callista's thoughts also drifted to Dorian and Theron. Dorian, with his warm smile and adventurous spirit. She felt drawn to him in a way she couldn't fully explain. And Theron, her trusted friend and advisor, always ready with a kind word or astute observation. Her heart felt torn between duty and desire.

Shaking her head, Callista paused and steadied herself against a stone pillar. Now was not the time for such ruminations. She needed to focus on the council meeting and finding the best way to protect her people. Whatever personal feelings she harbored would have to wait.

Callista resumed her brisk pace through the twisting corridors. Ahead, she could hear the rising murmur of voices as she approached the council chamber. She squared her shoulders and lifted her chin, ready to face whatever challenges lay ahead. For the sake of Thera, she would not falter.

"High Priestess Callista!" Ariadne's urgent voice echoed through the corridor as she rushed to Callista's side, her white robes billowing behind her. "I must speak with you!"

Callista turned, her brow furrowed with concern as she took in Ariadne's wide, fearful eyes. "What is it, Ariadne? What's happened?"

The young acolyte struggled to catch her breath, her hands trembling as she clutched at her bronze pendant. "The fishermen, they've returned with disturbing news. The fish, they're behaving even more strangely. Jumping out of the water, swimming in erratic patterns. Some even washing up on the shore, dead."

Callista's heart sank as she absorbed Ariadne's words. Another omen, and a troubling one at that. "Have you spoken to anyone else about this?"

Ariadne shook her head, her curly red hair escaping from beneath her veil. "No, I came straight to you. I know the council is gathering, and I thought you should know immediately."

"You did well, Ariadne," Callista said, placing a reassuring hand on the girl's shoulder. "I will bring this news to the council. We must act quickly to understand what the gods are trying to tell us."

As they approached the Temple council chamber, the air grew thick with tension. Raised voices and anxious murmurs filtered through the heavy wooden doors, punctuated by the occasional slight tremor that sent ripples of fear through the gathered priests and advisors. Callista paused at the threshold, her hand resting on the cool bronze handle. She glanced at Ariadne, who offered an encouraging nod, her eyes still wide with a mix of excitement and apprehension.

Drawing in a steadying breath, Callista pushed open the doors and stepped into the chamber. The room fell silent as all eyes turned to her, the weight of their expectations settling heavily on her shoulders.

She surveyed the gathered faces - the worried frowns of the elders, the tense jaws of the warriors, the hopeful gazes of the younger priests. In the flickering light of the bronze braziers, she could see the fear that lurked beneath their expressions, the unspoken questions that hung in the air.

"Friends, honored council members," Callista began, her voice clear and steady despite the unease that coiled in her stomach. "I come bearing troubling news. The omens are mounting, and we must act swiftly to help the people of Thera survive the cataclysm that is certainly coming."

As she spoke, Callista's mind raced with the implications of the strange fish behavior, the tremors, and the other signs that had plagued Thera in recent weeks. She knew that her next words could shape the fate of her people, and the weight of that responsibility settled heavily on her heart. But she was the High Priestess of Potnia, chosen by the gods to lead and guide her people. And with the support of those gathered in this room, she knew they could face whatever challenges lay ahead.

At the back of the room, Dorian watched Callista with a mixture of admiration and concern. He marveled at the way she commanded the attention of the council, her voice ringing with authority and grace despite the gravity of the situation. The incense-scented air seemed to shimmer around her, as if the very gods were lending their strength to her words.

But beneath his awe, Dorian's heart ached for the burden Callista carried. He longed to stand by her side, to offer his support and comfort in the face of the mounting crisis. His mind raced with possibilities, searching for ways he could help without overstepping his bounds as an outsider. Perhaps his knowledge of other cultures and his connections in distant ports really would prove useful in the days to come. If the worst came to pass and evacuation became necessary, his skills as a navigator and his familiarity with the sea could be invaluable. For now, though, all he could do was listen and observe, ready to lend his aid when the time was right. He caught Callista's eye from across the room, offering a small, reassuring smile that he hoped would convey his unwavering support.

Callista felt a flicker of warmth in her chest as she met Dorian's gaze, drawing strength from the quiet encouragement in his eyes. She took a deep breath, steadying herself before continuing.

"I propose that we send emissaries to the far reaches of the island, to gather more information on the extent of these omens. We must also consult the ancient texts and perform the necessary rituals to seek guidance from Potnia herself."

The council members murmured their assent, nodding solemnly as they absorbed Callista's words. The tension in the room seemed to ease slightly, replaced by a sense of purpose and determination. "We will begin preparing the people for the idea of imminent evacuation as well. We need to get them comfortable with the idea of leaving on short notice, and having provisions and a small amount of personal belongings ready to be grabbed at a moments notice." Callista looked at Captain Minoas Lysandros as she said this, he nodded in agreement.

"Together, we will weather this storm," Callista declared, her voice ringing with conviction. "Thera has stood strong for generations, and with the blessing of the gods, we shall endure."

As the council members began discussion ideas among themselves, their voices rising and falling in heated debate, Theron approached Callista, his brow furrowed with concern. "High Priestess," he began, his tone low and urgent, "I fear these omens may be more severe than we initially believed."

Callista turned to face him, her green eyes searching his face. "What have you seen, Brother Theron?"

Theron reached into his satchel, producing a handful of volcanic rocks, their surfaces glistening with strange, iridescent veins. "I discovered these near the summit," he explained, his voice trembling slightly. "I've never seen anything like them before. The mountain itself seems to be changing, as if awakening from a deep slumber."

Callista gently took the rocks from Theron's hand, turning them over in her palm. A chill ran down her spine as she traced the shimmering lines with her fingertip. "This is indeed troubling," she murmured, her mind racing with the implications.

Around them, the council members continued to argue, their voices growing louder and more insistent. "We must evacuate immediately!" one man shouted, his face flushed with fear. "The gods have abandoned us!"

"No!" another countered, slamming his fist on the table. "We must have faith! Potnia will protect her chosen people!"

Callista raised her hand, silencing the clamor. She turned to address the council members who remained, her bearing regal and composed. "Enough," she said, her voice firm but gentle. "We must not let fear cloud our judgment. We cannot make rash decisions."

As Callista moved about the chamber, Theron fell into step beside her, his voice low and confidential. "High Priestess, I volunteer to lead an expedition to the summit and back into the caves. I believe I can find the answers we seek."

Callista hesitated, her heart clenching at the thought of sending Theron into danger. But as she met his earnest gaze, she knew that he was the right choice. "Very well, Brother Theron," she said softly, placing a hand on his shoulder. "But promise me you will be careful. Thera needs your wisdom and courage now more than ever."

Theron bowed his head, a small smile tugging at the corners of his mouth. "I will not fail you, High Priestess. Or our people."

As he turned to leave, Callista watched him go, a sense of foreboding settling in her chest. The path ahead was shrouded in uncertainty, but she knew that they would face it together, guided by the light of Potnia and the strength of their own convictions.

The council chamber doors burst open right before Theron reached them, and Lykos strode in, his ornate robes billowing behind him. "High Priestess Callista!" he bellowed, his voice reverberating off the stone walls. "You stand accused of heresy and treason against the sacred traditions of Thera!"

Callista turned, her heart pounding in her chest. "Priest-King Lykos, what is the meaning of this intrusion?" she asked, her voice steady despite the fear coursing through her veins.

Lykos's eyes narrowed, his gaze sweeping over the assembled council members. "It has come to my attention that you have been spreading false prophecies and leading our people astray," he declared, his tone dripping with disdain. "Your visions are nothing more than the ravings of a madwoman, and your actions threaten the very foundation of our society."

Gasps of shock and outrage rippled through the room, and Callista could feel the weight of every gaze upon her. She took a deep breath, drawing on the strength of Potnia to steady her nerves. "My visions are a gift from the Great Mother herself," she said, her voice ringing with quiet conviction. "I have seen the signs of impending disaster, and it is my sacred duty to warn our people and guide them to safety."

Lykos scoffed, his lips curling into a sneer. "You dare to claim divine authority over the priest-king himself?" he demanded, his eyes flashing with barely contained fury. "Your arrogance knows no bounds, Callista. You have betrayed the trust of your people and the gods themselves."

The chamber erupted into a cacophony of voices, some defending Callista's integrity, others demanding answers and explanations. Through it all, Callista remained calm, her gaze locked with Lykos's in a silent battle of wills.

"I have betrayed no one," she said firmly, her voice cutting through the din. "I have only sought to serve Potnia and protect our people from the dangers that threaten us. If you cannot see the truth of my words, then perhaps it is you who have lost sight of the gods' will."

Lykos's face contorted with rage, and for a moment, Callista feared that he might strike her down where she stood. But instead, he drew himself up to his full height, his voice cold and unyielding. "We shall see what the gods have to say about your treachery," he hissed. "Mark my words, Callista. You will face judgment for your crimes, and Thera will be purged of your poisonous influence once and for all."

With that, he turned on his heel and stormed out of the chamber, leaving a stunned silence in his wake. Callista sank back into her seat, her mind reeling from the confrontation. She knew that Lykos's accusations were baseless, but she could not deny the fear that gripped her heart. The future of Thera hung in the balance, and she would need all of her strength and wisdom to guide her people through the trials to come.

Dorian watched as Lykos's accusations hung in the air, casting a pall over the council chamber. His heart ached for Callista, who stood tall and proud in the face of such venom. He longed to go to her, to wrap her in his arms and shield her from the world, but he knew that such a display would only fuel the rumors that swirled around them.

Instead, he remained rooted to the spot, his mind racing with the implications of Lykos's words. If the high priest truly believed that Callista was a traitor, then no one on Thera was safe from his wrath. Dorian's thoughts turned to the possibility of leaving the island, of taking Callista far away from the danger that threatened to engulf her.

But even as the idea took hold, he knew that he could not abandon her, and she would not abandon her people to leave with him not now, when they needed her most. Callista was more than just the woman he loved; she was the heart and soul of Thera, the one person who could guide them through the coming storm. To leave her now would be to betray everything he believed in, for her to leave with him would mean abandoning her life's work, her faith.

Theron, too, found himself torn between his loyalty to the temple and his faith in Callista. He had known her since they were children, had watched her grow into the wise and compassionate leader she was today. He could not believe that she would ever betray their people, no matter what Lykos claimed.

As the shock of the accusation began to wear off, Theron felt a surge of anger rise within him. How dare Lykos question Callista's devotion to Potnia, after all she had done for Thera? How dare he sow seeds of doubt and fear among the council, when unity was more important than ever?

Before he could stop himself, Theron turned to those in the chamber, his voice ringing out across the open space. "I have known Callista most of my life," he said, his gaze locked on Lykos's retreating form. "She is a true servant of the gods, and a leader of unparalleled wisdom and courage. To accuse her of treason is to spit in the face of all that is holy on Thera."

A murmur of agreement rippled through the crowd, and Theron felt a flicker of hope kindle in his chest. Perhaps, with the support of the council, Callista could weather this storm and lead them to safety. Perhaps, together, they could find a way to appease the gods and save their beloved island from destruction.

But even as he spoke, Theron knew that the road ahead would be long and perilous. Lykos's accusations had planted a seed of doubt in the minds of many, and it would take all of their strength and unity to overcome the challenges that lay ahead. For now, all he could do was stand by Callista's side and pray that the gods would guide them through the darkness to come.

Chapter 11: The Scroll of Aisforos

Ariadne's fingers fluttered over the ancient scrolls, her curiosity propelling her forward. The musty scent of the archives filled her nostrils as she searched, dust motes dancing in the dim light. Her heart raced with anticipation, the recent tremors that shook Thera spurring her on.

"It must be here somewhere," she muttered to herself, carefully shifting aside another stack of aging parchment. "The answers are in these scrolls, I just know it."

The distant crash of waves against the cliffs echoed faintly through the stone walls, a reminder of the powerful forces that shaped their island home. Ariadne paused, tilting her head to listen. The sea always seemed to whisper to her, even here in the depths of the temple.

With a determined nod, she returned to her task, her eyes scanning the shelves. And then, tucked behind a row of ceremonial texts, she spotted it - an ancient scroll, its edges cracked and yellowed with age. Ariadne's breath caught in her throat as she reached for it, her fingers trembling slightly. As she carefully pulled the scroll free, a thrill ran through her. The parchment felt delicate beneath her fingertips, the weight of history tangible in her hands. She brought it closer, inhaling the scent of centuries past, a mix of dust, aged leather, and the faintest hint of incense.

"Oh, this is old," she whispered reverently, her eyes widening as she gently unrolled the scroll. The script was faded and difficult to make out in the flickering lamplight, but Ariadne leaned closer, squinting at the ancient characters. Her heart pounded in her ears as she made out the first few lines.

The shadows seemed to dance around her as she read on, the world fading away until only she and the scroll existed. Each word felt charged with significance, a piece of a puzzle she was desperate to solve. With bated breath, Ariadne lost herself in the ancient text, the crash of waves and the crumbling scroll her only companions in the dusty archive.

Ariadne's heart raced with excitement as she read the prophecy, her fingers tracing over the faded words on the ancient scroll. The more she read, the more her excitement grew. It was a tale of great calamity, of destruction that would befall their beloved Thera. But it also spoke of hope - of a chosen triad who held the key to salvation.

Ariadne took a deep breath before beginning to read the text again, but aloud this time. As she spoke, the chamber fell silent, each word resonating with an eerie weight. The prophecy foretold of a time when Thera would suffer great destruction - earthquakes, fires and floods that would ravage their island home.

"But there is hope," Ariadne said aloud. "For it speaks of a chosen triad who will bring balance and peace back to our land."

Her voice trembled with emotion as she read of a young woman from within their own rank of priestesses - a pure-hearted priestess who possessed wisdom beyond her years, a sailor whose strength and courage would be unrivaled, and a seer from a rival temple with visions that could guide them towards salvation.

The room was quiet as a tomb at this revelation. Her mind raced, connecting the dots between the recent tremors and the dire warnings etched in ink. Connecting the dots about the triad it mentions.

"By the gods," she breathed, her voice echoing in the empty room. "This changes everything."

Ariadne rolled the scroll carefully, her fingers trembling with a mixture of exhilaration and trepidation. She knew she had to share this discovery with Callista, Dorian, and Theron immediately. They would know what to do, how to interpret the prophecy and guide Thera through the impending crisis.

Clutching the scroll to her chest, Ariadne rushed out of the archives, her sandals slapping against the cool stone floors. She navigated the winding corridors of the temple with practiced ease, her white robes billowing behind her as she hurried towards the inner sanctum where she knew the trio would be gathered.

As she burst into the room, three pairs of eyes turned to her, curiosity and concern mingling in their gazes. Ariadne's cheeks were flushed, her red curls escaping from beneath her veil in wild tendrils. She opened her mouth to speak, but the words tumbled out in an excited rush.

"I found something," she panted, holding up the scroll like a sacred offering. "A prophecy, ancient and powerful. It speaks of Thera's destruction and a chosen triad who can save us."

Callista, Dorian, and Theron exchanged glances, their expressions shifting from surprise to intrigue. Ariadne's enthusiasm was infectious, her eyes sparkling with the thrill of discovery. She could barely contain herself as she crossed the room, her voice rising with each step.

"You must read it," she insisted, pressing the scroll into Callista's hands. "It's all here, the key to our future. The gods have spoken, and we must listen."

As the trio huddled around the ancient parchment, Ariadne's heart swelled with pride and purpose. She knew, deep in her bones, that this was the moment they had been waiting for, the catalyst that would set them on the path to destiny. The musty scent of the scroll mingled with the sweet aroma of burning incense, a tangible reminder of the sacred trust they bore.

Callista's brow furrowed as she studied the ancient text, her green eyes scanning each line with a mix of reverence and intensity. She spoke softly, her words measured and thoughtful. "The Scroll of Aisforos, the bringer of ash. A dire warning, to be sure, but also a glimmer of hope. The gods have chosen us for a reason."

Dorian leaned in closer, his curiosity piqued. "But what does it mean, exactly? How are we supposed to save Thera from destruction?" He ran a hand through his tousled hair, his warm smile tinged with a hint of concern.

Theron, ever the analytical mind, peered over Callista's shoulder, his ink-stained fingers tracing the edges of the scroll. "We must approach this carefully," he cautioned, his voice steady and precise. "The prophecy is clear, but the path forward is not. We need to study this further, to understand the implications before we act."

Ariadne bounced on her toes, her impatience palpable. "But we can't wait too long! The tremors, the signs, they all point to something big happening soon. We have to be ready."

Callista placed a gentle hand on Ariadne's shoulder, her touch calming the young priestess's restless energy. "Ariadne, your enthusiasm is a gift, but Theron is right. We must proceed with wisdom and caution. The gods have entrusted us with this knowledge for a reason, and we must not take it lightly."

Dorian nodded, his eyes sparkling with a mix of excitement and determination. "We'll figure this out together, as a team. The prophecy chose us for a reason, and I believe in our strength, our unity."

A heavy silence descended upon the room, the weight of the prophecy settling over the group like a tangible presence. Callista, Dorian, and Theron exchanged meaningful glances, each grappling with the profound implications of the ancient words and their own roles within the unfolding destiny of Thera. The air seemed to thicken with tension and uncertainty, the only sound being the soft rustling of the scroll as Ariadne carefully rolled it up, her fingers trembling slightly.

Callista's mind raced, her thoughts tumbling over one another like the restless waves of the Aegean Sea. As the High Priestess, she felt the burden of responsibility pressing upon her shoulders, the need to guide her people through the challenges that lay ahead. Yet, beneath the mantle of her sacred duty, a flicker of doubt emerged, a whisper of uncertainty about the path that the gods had laid before them.

Dorian's eyes shone with a mix of wonder and apprehension, his curiosity piqued by the cryptic words of the prophecy. He leaned forward, his voice low and earnest, "What does this mean for us, for

Thera? Are we truly the chosen ones destined to face this 'bringer of ash'?"

Theron remained silent, his brow furrowed in deep contemplation. The analytical skeptic within him grappled with the otherworldly nature of the prophecy, seeking to unravel its mysteries through the lens of logic and reason. Yet, even he could not deny the palpable sense of destiny that hung in the air, the feeling that their lives had been inexorably altered by the discovery of the ancient scroll.

Just as Callista opened her mouth to speak, the heavy wooden door of the chamber swung open with a resounding thud. Lykos Theodoros strode into the room, his presence commanding and authoritative, his ornate robes swirling around him like a tempest. His steely gray eyes immediately fixed upon Callista, a mixture of suspicion and challenge flickering within their depths.

"High Priestess Callista," Lykos's voice cut through the tension like a knife, his tone sharp and demanding. "I have been informed of a most unusual disturbance within the temple archives. Whispers of a prophecy, a scroll of great significance." He extended his hand, palm up, his fingers beckoning impatiently. "Surrender the scroll to me, immediately."

Callista felt her heartbeat quicken, a sudden rush of adrenaline coursing through her veins. She met Lykos's gaze unflinchingly, her own eyes reflecting a quiet strength and determination. "High Priest Lykos," she began, her voice steady and calm, belying the tumult of emotions within her. "The scroll speaks of matters that concern the very fate of Thera. It is not a mere trinket to be passed around lightly."

Lykos's eyes narrowed, his jaw clenching with barely contained irritation. "You forget yourself, High Priestess. The temple archives are under my jurisdiction, and any matters of prophecy must be brought before the council for proper interpretation and action." He took a step closer, his imposing figure looming over Callista. "I will not ask again. Give me the scroll."

"How are you even aware we have this scroll? Ariadne only just brought it to us." Dorian demanded to know. The three glanced at Ariadne who looked confused, but then realized the implication.

"I did not tell a single person about the scroll!" Araidne glared at them.

"You need not tell anyone, I have eyes and ears everywhere on Thera young one." Lykos' meaning clear to them. He had spies watching them.

Dorian and Theron instinctively moved closer to Callista, their presence a silent show of support and protection. Dorian's warm brown eyes held a glint of defiance as he spoke, his voice measured yet firm. "With all due respect, Priest-King Lykos, the prophecy speaks of a chosen triad. It is our duty to understand its meaning before presenting it to the council."

Lykos's gaze snapped to Dorian, a flicker of disdain crossing his features. "Ah, the foreign diplomat speaks out of turn. Your opinion holds little weight within these sacred walls, Dorian Xenophon." He turned his attention back to Callista, his voice dripping with condescension. "And you, High Priestess, would you truly place your faith in the ravings of an ancient scroll over the wisdom of the council?"

Callista's grip tightened on the scroll, the parchment crinkling beneath her fingers. She drew in a steady breath, her mind racing as she carefully chose her next words. "The prophecy speaks of Aisforos, the bringer of ash. It warns of a great calamity that threatens to engulf Thera. We cannot ignore the signs, Sire. The very earth trembles beneath our feet."

Lykos scoffed, a harsh, mirthless sound that echoed through the room. "Superstitious nonsense. The earth trembles because the gods are displeased with your defiance, High Priestess. Your actions border on heresy, and I will not stand for it."

Theron stepped forward, his voice quiet but resolute. "Priest-King Lykos, as one who has studied the earth-signs, I can assure you that these tremors are no ordinary occurrence. The prophecy merits further investigation, for the safety and well-being of our people."

Lykos's gaze swept over the trio, his expression hardening with each passing moment. "I see you are all determined to undermine my authority. Very well, keep your precious scroll for now. But know this—your actions will have consequences. The council will hear of your insubordination, and the gods will judge your faithlessness harshly."

With a final, withering glare, Lykos turned on his heel and strode out of the room, his ceremonial robes billowing behind him. The heavy door slammed shut, the sound reverberating through the suddenly silent space.

Callista released a shaky breath, her heart pounding in her ears. She looked to Dorian and Theron, gratitude and determination mingling in her eyes. "Thank you, both of you, for standing with me. But Lykos's warning is not to be taken lightly. We must tread carefully and seek the truth behind this prophecy, for the sake of Thera and all who call this island home."

Dorian nodded, his warm brown eyes filled with concern. "Callista is right. We've stepped onto a dangerous path, but we can't turn back now. The prophecy spoke of a chosen triad, and I believe that's us. We have to see this through, no matter the cost."

Theron ran a hand through his ink-stained fingers, his brow furrowed in thought. "But what if Lykos is right? What if we're misinterpreting the signs, and our actions bring more harm than good? The council's judgment is not to be taken lightly, and the gods' wrath is a fearsome thing."

Callista placed a gentle hand on Theron's shoulder, her voice soft but firm. "I understand your fears, Theron. But in my heart, I know this is the path we must follow. The Great Mother has guided us to this moment, and we must trust in her wisdom."

She unrolled the ancient scroll once more, her fingers tracing the faded ink. "The prophecy speaks of a great calamity, but also of hope. We have been chosen to face this challenge, and I believe that together, we can find a way to save our people."

Dorian leaned in, his eyes scanning the cryptic text. "Aisforos, the bringer of ash. Could it be referring to the mountain? The tremors, the smoke rising from the peak—it all points to something brewing beneath the surface."

Theron's eyes widened, his analytical mind whirring. "If that's true, then we have even less time than we thought. We need to learn more about this prophecy, to understand what we're up against and how we can stop it."

Callista nodded, determination etched across her face. "Then that's what we'll do. We'll study the scroll, search the archives for any related texts, and seek guidance from the gods. But we must be discreet. Lykos will be watching our every move, waiting for a chance to discredit us."

Dorian grinned, his natural charisma shining through. "Leave that to me. I have made more than a few friends in the city who might be able to help us gather information without drawing too much attention. We'll need all the allies we can get if we're going to pull this off."

Callista, Dorian, and Theron stepped out of the temple archives, the ancient scroll carefully concealed beneath Callista's flowing robes. The warm Aegean sun embraced them, its golden rays a stark contrast to the cool, musty air of the archives. The weight of their decision hung heavy in the air, a palpable presence that seemed to follow them like a shadow.

Callista paused at the top of the stone steps, her green eyes scanning the bustling streets of Pyrgos Kallistis below. The distant sounds of merchants haggling and children laughing drifted up to them, a bittersweet reminder of the carefree lives they were leaving behind.

"We can't let them down," Callista said softly, her voice tinged with determination. "Our people, our island... they're counting on us, even if they don't know it yet."

Dorian placed a comforting hand on her shoulder, his warm smile a beacon of hope in the midst of their uncertainty. "And we won't," he assured her. "We'll face this together, no matter what comes our way."

Theron nodded, his brow furrowed in thought. "But we must be cautious. Lykos will stop at nothing to maintain his power, and if he discovers what we know..."

"He won't," Callista said firmly, her fingers tightening around the scroll. "We'll keep this between us until we know more. In the meantime, we have work to do."

As they descended the steps, the trio exchanged glances, their expressions a mix of excitement, fear, and determination. The path ahead was shrouded in mystery, but one thing was certain: they were in this together, bound by fate and a shared purpose that would guide them through the challenges to come.

The sun-drenched streets of Pyrgos Kallistis stretched out before them, a tapestry of white stone and vibrant life. With each step, they felt the weight of their destiny pressing down upon them, a constant reminder of the task that lay ahead. But as they walked, shoulders squared and heads held high, they knew that they were ready to face whatever the future held, armed with the power of the prophecy and the strength of their unbreakable bond.

Chapter 12: Trial by Fire

The agora hummed with anticipation, a sea of faces turned towards the makeshift platform that stood at its heart. Merchants and craftsmen, fishermen and farmers, all had gathered to witness the trial that would decide the fate of their beloved high priestess. They jostled for position, craning their necks and murmuring in low tones.

"Is it true what they say?" a weathered sailor asked his companion. "That she prophesied doom for us all?"

"Hush now," the other man replied, his eyes fixed on the platform. "The gods will decide her fate, not idle gossip."

A hush fell over the crowd as a figure emerged from the temple, her robes shimmering in the morning light. High Priestess Callista moved with practiced grace, her bearing regal yet humble. As she ascended the steps to the platform, Callista took in the faces of her people - faces etched with worry, with fear, with hope.

She closed her eyes for a moment, offering a silent prayer to Potnia. 'Mother Goddess, guide my words. Let me speak truth and bring comfort to your children.' Opening her eyes, Callista stood tall and faced the assembled Therans.

"People of Thera," she began, her voice carrying across the agora. "I stand before you today not as your judge, but as your servant. The visions granted to me by the Great Mother are not a curse, but a warning. A chance for us to prepare and protect our people."

Callista paused, letting her words sink in. She saw a mix of emotions playing across the faces in the crowd - doubt, fear, but also a tentative trust. They had always looked to her for guidance, and she would not abandon them now.

"I know these are uncertain times. But we Therans have weathered storms before, and together, we shall weather this one too. Let us put our faith in the gods, and in each other." Callista held out her hands in a gesture of unity. "Now more than ever, we must stand as one people, one family. As children of Potnia, we are never alone."

As Callista stepped back from the podium, a murmur rippled through the crowd. Some faces shone with rekindled hope; others remained clouded by doubts. But all eyes were fixed on the woman who had the power to command seismic change for their island. What would she say in her defense? What fate awaited Thera under her guidance? Only the gods could say for certain. The people of the agora held their collective breath, waiting for the trial to unfold.

Lykos stepped forward, his ceremonial robes swirling around him like a gathering storm. He cast a sharp gaze over the assembled crowd, his voice ringing out with the clarity of a bronze bell. "People of Thera, hear me now. The words of our High Priestess may be honeyed, but they drip with the poison of falsehood."

He turned to face Callista directly, his eyes narrowing. "You speak of warnings and preparation, yet your visions have sown only discord and unrest. How can we trust the ravings of a mind touched by madness?"

Callista met his accusation with an unwavering stare. "It is not madness that guides my visions, Lykos, but the divine breath of Potnia herself. I have dedicated my life to interpreting her sacred signs, and I will not be cowed by your baseless attacks."

Lykos scoffed, his lips curling into a sneer. "Sacred signs? Or self-serving delusions? The people of Thera deserve a leader who speaks with reason, not one who whispers of doom and destruction. One who preaches abandonement of our homes!"

"And what reason do you offer, Lykos?" Callista countered, her voice steady and strong. "The reason of a man who clings to power at any cost? The reason of a priest who would silence the voice of the Mother to maintain his own authority?"

A murmur rippled through the crowd at her bold words. Lykos's face flushed with anger, but he quickly smoothed his features into a mask of paternal concern. "I offer the reason of tradition, High Priestess. The reason of stability and order. Your visions threaten to upend the very foundations of our society. You wish to see us leave our home and never return."

Callista shook her head, her eyes softening as she addressed the crowd once more. "My friends, my family, I stand before you not to bring chaos, but to offer clarity. The visions granted to me by Potnia are a gift, a chance for us to safeguard our civilization, our families, our friends, our traditions, and our future."

She took a step closer to the edge of the platform, her voice resonating with quiet conviction. "I ask not for blind faith, but for open hearts and minds. Let us work together to prepare for whatever challenges may come. As your High Priestess, my duty is to guide and protect, never to deceive."

Lykos opened his mouth to retort, but Callista held up a hand, silencing him. "The choice lies with you, people of Thera. Will you cling to the comfort of the known, even as the earth trembles beneath our feet? Or will you embrace the wisdom of the Mother, and walk the path of resilience and unity?"

As her words faded into the charged air, the crowd erupted into a cacophony of voices, some shouting support, others hurling questions and doubts. Callista stood amidst the chaos, a beacon of serenity, her faith in her people and her purpose unwavering. The trial had only just begun, but she knew in her heart that the truth would prevail, no matter the cost.

As the clamor of the crowd swelled, Dorian Xenophon stepped forward, his sun-bronzed features etched with determination. The sea-green of his tunic caught the sunlight as he moved, a vibrant contrast to the earthen tones of the agora. With a fluid gesture, he raised his hands, and the crowd's murmurs gradually subsided, drawn by his magnetic presence.

"People of Thera," Dorian began, his voice warm and resonant, "I come before you not as a stranger, but as a friend. In my travels across the wide-blue seas, I have witnessed the wisdom of many cultures, the strength that comes from embracing change and adaptation."

He paused, his gaze sweeping over the gathered faces, meeting their eyes with a genuine connection. "The visions of your esteemed High Priestess are not to be feared, but to be heeded. In distant lands, I have seen the signs of nature's unrest, and the resilience of those who listen to her warnings. I have seen the result of the hubris of those who ignore those warnings as well! Your people saved my life, now all I want is to return the favor."

"We stand at a crossroads, my friends. The choice between clinging to the familiar and the choice of embracing the wisdom of change. Lykos speaks of tradition, of the comfort of the known. But in a world where the very earth shifts beneath our feet, is it not your duty to evolve, to grow?"

As Dorian spoke, the crowd's energy began to shift, whispers of agreement rippling through the sea of faces. Some nodded, their eyes alight with newfound understanding, while others furrowed their brows, torn between the pull of tradition and the allure of Dorian's words.

Lykos, his jaw clenched, watched the crowd's reaction with growing unease. The charismatic seafarer's words were a direct challenge to his authority, his carefully constructed narrative of stability and control.

Dorian, sensing the crowd's divided loyalties, pressed on, his tone gentle yet insistent. "The Mother's signs are not a punishment, but a gift. A chance for you to adapt, to build a future that honors your past while embracing the ever-changing present."

He turned to Callista, a smile of respect and support playing on his lips. "Your High Priestess is a beacon of wisdom and compassion. Let us stand with her, united in your commitment to the well-being of theTheran people."

As Dorian's words faded into the charged air, the crowd's reaction was a mixture of excitement and uncertainty. Some cheered, their voices rising in support of the seafarer's message, while others murmured among themselves, their doubts not yet fully assuaged.

Dorian stepped back, his eyes meeting Callista's in a silent exchange of gratitude and solidarity. The trial was far from over, but his testimony had sown the seeds of change, challenging the rigid traditions that Lykos so fiercely defended. In the face of the gathering storm, both literal and figurative, the people of Thera stood at a precipice, their fate hanging in the balance. The choices they made in the coming moments would shape not only their own lives but the very future of their sacred isle.

As the murmurs of the crowd swelled in the wake of Dorian's testimony, Theron stepped forward, his inkstained fingers clutching a sheaf of parchment. The young priest's eyes, usually alight with curiosity, now shone with a solemn determination as he faced the gathered Therans.

"People of Thera," Theron began, his voice carrying a quiet authority, "I come before you not only as a servant of the Mother but as a student of Her sacred mysteries. In my studies, I have seen the signs that High Priestess Callista speaks of, written in the very earth beneath our feet."

He unrolled the parchment, revealing intricate sketches of the mountain, its slopes marked with meticulous notations. "The tremors that shake our houses, the noxious gases that rises from the cracks in the rock—these are not random occurrences but a pattern, a language that the Mother uses to communicate with Her children."

Theron's finger traced a line on the sketch, his voice growing more impassioned. "Each quake, each wisp of smoke, is a piece of a greater message, a warning that we ignore at our peril."

As he spoke, Theron's eyes met those of the gathered Therans, his gaze imploring them to see the truth in his words. "We have a choice before us, a chance to heed the Mother's call and prepare for the challenges that lie ahead. To build a future that is resilient, adaptable, and in harmony with the sacred forces that shape our world. But to do that we must leave this place. If we do not, we will certainly perish here, erased from history."

The crowd's reaction was a tapestry of emotions, their faces a mix of awe, uncertainty, and growing realization. Some nodded slowly, their eyes widening as they absorbed Theron's words, while others exchanged glances, their expressions shifting from skepticism to a dawning comprehension.

Theron's voice softened, his tone becoming more reflective. "In my studies, I have seen the cycles of the gods wrath, the ebb and flow of the Mother's breath. Change is not to be feared but embraced, for it is through change that we grow, that we become more than we were before."

He turned to Callista, his expression one of deep respect and support. "Our High Priestess is not a harbinger of doom but a messenger of hope, a guide who can lead us through the trials that lie ahead. Let us stand with her, united in our faith and our commitment to the well-being of Thera and her people."

As Theron's words faded into the charged air, the tension in the agora reached a fever pitch, the crowd's emotions a swirling maelstrom of doubt and belief. Some voices rose in support of the young priest's message, while others clung to their traditional views, their uncertainty a palpable presence in the sun-drenched square.

Lykos, his eyes narrowing as he surveyed the shifting tide of the crowd's sentiment, stepped forward once more. His voice, now tinged with a desperate edge, rose above the murmurs. "People of Thera, do not be swayed by the honeyed words of a misguided youth, a foreign devil, and a priestess who claims to speak for the gods. Their lies threaten the very foundation of our sacred traditions!"

He gestured accusingly at Callista, his robes billowing in the growing breeze. "This woman's visions are nothing more than the fevered imaginings of a mind unhinged. She seeks to sow discord and chaos, to tear apart the very fabric of our society for her own gain."

Callista stood her ground, her voice calm and steady in the face of Lykos's onslaught. "I speak only the truth, as revealed to me by the Mother herself. I have no desire for power or control, only a deep love for our people and a commitment to their well-being."

Lykos scoffed, his lips curling into a sneer. "Love? Commitment? These are mere words, easily spoken but rarely acted upon. Your actions, High Priestess, speak louder than any hollow sentiment. You would lead us astray, down a path of ruin and destruction."

As the two figures clashed, their words a battleground of conviction and accusation, the earth beneath their feet began to tremble. At first, it was a subtle vibration, barely noticeable amidst the din of the trial. But as the seconds ticked by, the tremors grew in intensity, sending ripples of fear through the assembled crowd. Panic erupted as the ground heaved and buckled, the ancient stones of the agora shifting and cracking under the force of the quake. People stumbled and fell, their screams of terror piercing the air as they sought to flee the collapsing platform and the raining debris.

Callista, her heart pounding in her chest, reached out to steady a nearby woman, her eyes scanning the chaos for signs of Dorian and Theron. She knew, with a sinking certainty, that this was only the beginning of the calamity she had foreseen. The Mother's warning had come to pass, and now, more than ever, her people needed her guidance and strength.

As the dust began to settle and the tremors subsided, Callista stood tall amidst the rubble, her voice rising above the frightened sobs and urgent shouts. "People of Thera, hear me now! This is the moment we have feared, the moment we must face together. Let us not be divided by fear and doubt, but united in our love for this sacred land and our faith in the Mother's wisdom."

Dorian emerged from the settling dust, his strong frame helping those who had been knocked off their feet. His voice joined Callista's, carrying across the agora with a reassuring calm. "The high priestess speaks the truth! We must set aside our differences and work as one to ensure the safety of our people. Let us look to the wisdom of your leaders and the strength of your community. You Therans are great sailors, fishermen, and merchants! Ply the waves and find a new home, a safe haven, for your people!"

Theron, his analytical mind already assessing the damage, moved swiftly to Callista's side. "The tremors have weakened the foundations of the buildings nearby," he said, his voice low but urgent. "We must guide the people to open ground, away from anything that might collapse."

Callista nodded, her eyes meeting Theron's with a silent understanding. She turned back to the crowd, her voice clear and commanding. "Follow Theron's lead! Move calmly and quickly to the park beyond the Agora's center. There, we will regroup and decide our next course of action."

As the people began to move, their initial panic giving way to a fragile sense of purpose, a collective gasp rippled through the crowd. All eyes turned to the distant peak of the sacred mountain, where a plume of dark smoke had begun to rise, staining the clear blue sky with an ominous haze.

Callista felt a chill run down her spine, the sight confirming her deepest fears. The Mother's warning had not been just about the earthquake, but about the very heart of the island awakening with a fury that threatened to consume them all.

"The mountain," Dorian whispered, his voice tinged with awe and trepidation. "It's just as you foresaw, Callista. The mountain is awakened. Aisforos comes."

The high priestess nodded solemnly, her gaze fixed on the distant peak. "The signs have been there all along, but now there can be no doubt. We stand on the brink of a great cataclysm, one that will test the very fabric of our society and our faith."

Callista stood tall amidst the manicured garden of the park, her dark hair whipping in the wind as she surveyed the faces around her. Gone were the skeptical looks and murmurs of doubt that had greeted her prophecies mere moments ago. In their place, she saw a mix of fear, awe, and a growing respect for the power of her visions.

Dorian moved to stand beside her, his hand resting reassuringly on her shoulder. "You were right all along, Callista," he said softly, his warm brown eyes filled with admiration. "The people see that now."

Callista nodded, a small smile playing at the corners of her lips. "It's not about being right, Dorian. It's about guiding our people through this crisis, and ensuring that we emerge stronger and wiser on the other side."

Theron approached them, his youthful face etched with concern. "The earthquake was just the beginning," he said, his voice low and urgent. "If the volcano erupts, it could mean disaster for all of Thera."

"Then we must act quickly," Callista replied, her gaze sweeping over the crowd once more. She raised her voice, addressing the people with a calm authority that belied the urgency of the situation. "People of Thera, hear me now. The Mother has spoken, and we must heed her warning." She pointed to the small cloud of dark smoke rising from the mountain at their islands center. "Aisforos has awakened. We must prepare for departure from this island."

"You will not face this alone," Dorian added, his voice ringing out across the assembly. "Together, we are strong, together we can move your people to new lands."

A murmur of agreement rippled through the crowd, and Callista felt a surge of pride in her people. They were resilient, adaptable, and deeply connected to the land and the gods. With leaders like Dorian and Theron by her side, she knew that they could face whatever challenges lay ahead.

Chapter 13: Exodus

The bustling agora pulsed with chaos as Callista, Dorian, and Theron stood at its edge, their eyes darting back and forth, surveying the frantic scene. Townspeople rushed about in a frenzy, gathering what meager belongings they could carry and shouting to one another with rising panic in their voices.

Callista's brow furrowed with concern. "We must act quickly to restore order," she said, her voice steady despite the turmoil surrounding them. "Theron, see if you can find Captain Minoas at the harbor. We'll need his ships and men to aid the evacuation."

Theron nodded, his keen eyes already mapping the most efficient path through the agora. "I'll ensure the vessels are prepared and coordinate the boarding." He hurried off, his lean frame disappearing into the crowd.

Dorian placed a reassuring hand on Callista's shoulder. "I'll help direct people to the harbor and keep them as calm as possible along the way." His warm smile belied the urgency in his eyes.

"Thank you, Dorian." Callista drew in a deep breath, centering herself. "I will address the crowd and provide what guidance I can."

With that, Callista stepped forward, her graceful movements and sacred ribbons catching the eye of the nearest townspeople. They began to still, their attention drawn to the High Priestess as if by an invisible force. Callista raised her hands, her voice ringing out clear and commanding across the agora.

"People of Thera!" The crowd's murmurs died down, faces turning toward Callista with a mix of fear and hope. "I know you are frightened, but we must remain orderly if we are to survive. Follow the evacuation plan, make your way to the harbor. Trust in the guidance of Potnia, the Great Mother, who watches over us even now."

As Callista spoke, a sense of calm seemed to ripple through the damaged agora. Her words, imbued with spiritual authority, settled over the townspeople like a soothing balm. In her presence, they found a glimmer of hope amidst the panic, their trust in the High Priestess and their belief in Potnia's protection temporarily quelling their fears.

"Move quickly, but calmly," Callista continued, her eyes meeting those of the people nearest her. "Help one another, and remember, we are all children of Potnia. She will guide us to safety." With a final nod of encouragement, Callista stepped back, allowing the newly focused crowd to begin their orderly procession towards the harbor and the promise of escape.

***

Dorian wove through the crowd, his warm smile and easy manner a beacon of reassurance amidst the chaos. He knelt beside a crying child, gently wiping away her tears. "Hey there, little one," he said softly, "I know it's scary, but we're going on an adventure together. We'll sail across the sea to a new place, just like the heroes in the stories. What do you say, want to be brave with me?"

The girl sniffled, nodding hesitantly as Dorian took her hand. He looked up at her mother, who clutched a bundle of hastily gathered belongings. "The ships are sturdy, and the sailors know these waters well. We'll make sure everyone has a safe place on board." He gestured towards the harbor, his experience with maritime logistics shining through as he explained, "The larger vessels will take on as many as they can, and the fishing boats will ferry people to Akrotiri if needed to get onto other ships. We have a plan, and we'll see it through together."

One of the elders stepped forward, his voice trembling, "But this is our home, foreign sailor! We've built our lives here, in the shadow of the sacred mountain. How can we leave it all behind?"

Another man stepped forward. "We are not wanderers, lost on the sea like you."

Dorian placed a comforting hand on the elder's shoulder, his eyes filled with compassion, even as the words of these men stung. "I know it's difficult," he said gently, "but the signs from the earth cannot be ignored. The mountain, as much as you revere it, poses a grave danger now." He paused, letting his words sink in before continuing, "It is not the buildings or the land that make a home, but the people. If you stay, you risk losing everything, including each other. Have faith in High Priestess Callista, and Captain Minoas, they have a plan to save you all."

The elders exchanged glances, their expressions shifting from fear to reluctant acceptance. Dorian pressed on, his voice firm but kind, "We must prioritize the safety of your community, your families, above all else. The temple will endure, as will your faith, as long as you stand together." He smiled softly, extending his hand, "The temple is not a building, a temple is the people."

As the elders began to follow Dorian towards the harbor, a glimmer of hope flickered in their eyes. They whispered prayers to Potnia, drawing strength from their faith and the unity of their people in the face of this unprecedented challenge.

***

Theron found Minoas in the harbor, just as he expected. Captain Minoas stood at the heart of the organized chaos. His deep voice boomed above the clamor of the crowd, "Load the provisions first, then the passengers. Keep the children towards the center of the deck." He gestured to a group of sailors, "You there, ensure the elderly have assistance boarding."

Minoas moved through the throng with purpose, his keen eyes surveying the progress of the evacuation. He paused to help a young mother navigate the narrow gangplank, her infant tucked securely in her arms. "Mind your step," he cautioned, offering a steadying hand. The woman nodded gratefully, whispering a prayer for his kindness.

As the captain turned to oversee the next vessel, a group of volunteers approached, their arms laden with blankets and water skins.

"Where should we distribute these, Captain?" a young man asked, his eyes wide with a mix of fear and determination.

Minoas clapped him on the shoulder, a flicker of a smile on his weathered face. "Good lad. See that every ship has a fair share. We've got a long journey ahead." He cast a glance at the darkening sky, the distant rumble of the mountain a constant reminder of the urgency of their mission.

Across the harbor, High Priestess Callista found herself surrounded by a group of townspeople, their voices rising in protest. "Priestess, we cannot abandon our homes, our sacred places," a woman cried, her face etched with distress. Others murmured in agreement, their fear palpable in the charged air.

Callista raised her hands, her presence emanating a calming energy. "My friends," she began, her tone soothing yet firm, "I understand your hesitation. Our connection to this land runs deep, as does our faith in Potnia." She met each of their gazes, her eyes reflecting their pain. "But we must remember, Potnia's love for her children extends beyond any single place. She is with us, guiding us to safety."

A man stepped forward, his voice trembling, "What if the mountain is a test of our devotion? What if leaving angers the gods?" Callista reached out, grasping his hands in her own, recognizing the false claims of Lykos on his lips. "The gods have spoken through the signs in the earth and sky. This is not a test, but a warning born of divine love. We must trust in their guidance and in each other."

***

Theron and Dorian weaved through the bustling harbor, Therons brow furrowed as he surveyed the scene. The ships were filling up fast, and the line of waiting evacuees still stretched far down the docks. He approached Captain Minoas, who was directing the loading of a large merchant vessel.

"Captain, we're running out of space," Theron said, his voice strained.

"There are still hundreds waiting to board." Dorian added.

Minoas wiped the sweat from his brow, his eyes never leaving the ship. "We're filling every inch, but you're right. We need more vessels."

Dorian's gaze swept the harbor, landing on a cluster of fishing boats bobbing gently in the waves. A spark of an idea ignited in his mind. He turned to Minoas, a grin spreading across his face. "The fishing boats. They may not be large, but they're seaworthy. If we can convince the fishermen to help..."

Minoas nodded, a glimmer of hope in his eyes. "It's worth a shot. Go, talk to them. I'll keep things moving here."

Dorian raced down the docks, his sandals slapping against the weathered wood. He approached a group of fishermen, their sun-weathered faces etched with worry as they watched the chaos unfold.

Theron turned to Minoas, "We may need to divert people to Akrotiri."

"Perhaps," Minoas sighed, "I hoped we wouldn't need to, that is a longer trek over land than I would want people to take now that Aisforos has awoken." He stared up at the mountain and felt true, gut-wrenching fear for one of the few times in his life. "But, we did plan for that possibility."

"Friends," Dorian called out, his voice carrying over the din as he approached the fishermen, "I know you're afraid, but we need your help. Your boats may be the difference between life and death for many."

The fishermen exchanged uncertain glances, until one, a grizzled man with a salt-and-pepper beard, stepped forward. "Our boats are small, made for nets, not crowds. How can we help?"

Dorian placed a hand on the man's shoulder, his eyes earnest. "Every space matters. We'll work together, find a way to safely load as many as we can. Your knowledge of the sea is invaluable now."

The fisherman's eyes softened, and he turned to his companions. "The young man's right. We can't turn our backs on our people." A murmur of agreement rippled through the group.

The fishermen sprang into action, preparing their small boats, throwing nets, baskets, and traps over the side, making as much room as possible on their small vessels. Theron stood at the edge of the barely organized chaos, his eyes fixed on a distant figure. Lykos, flanked by his most devoted followers, was making his way towards the mountain path, their faces set with grim determination.

Theron's heart raced, torn between the duty to help with the evacuation and the urge to confront Lykos. He knew the priest's intentions were misguided, rooted in a desperate attempt to cling to power in the face of disaster.

For a moment, Theron took a step forward, ready to chase after Lykos and make him see reason. But a cry from the harbor pulled his attention back - a child, separated from her family in the chaos, her face streaked with tears.

Theron's hesitation melted away. His place was here, helping those in need. Lykos's folly would have to run its course. With a heavy sigh, Theron turned back to the harbor, his voice joining the others as they called out to the frightened child, offering comfort amidst the turmoil.

The harbor was a scene of controlled chaos as Callista, Dorian, and Theron regrouped near the water's edge. Fishing boats bobbed alongside the larger vessels, their decks crowded with anxious evacuees. The trio exchanged weary smiles, their faces etched with a mix of determination and concern.

"The fishermen came through," Dorian said, his voice hoarse from shouting over the din. "But even with the extra boats, I fear we're cutting it close."

Callista nodded, her eyes scanning the throng of people still waiting on the docks. "We must prioritize the most vulnerable. Children, the elderly, those with infirmities."

Theron's brow furrowed as he mentally calculated the available space. "It's going to be tight, but I think we can manage. We'll have to be efficient with the loading, make sure every inch of deck space is used."

A woman's cry pierced through the clamor, drawing their attention. An elderly woman clutched at the arm of a young man, her face twisted with anguish. "Please, you must take my grandson! I'm too old, too slow. He's all I have left."

The young man shook his head vehemently, tears glistening in his eyes. "No, Grandmother. I won't leave you behind."

Callista's heart clenched as she watched the scene unfold. She glanced at Dorian and Theron, their expressions mirroring her own inner turmoil. They knew they couldn't save everyone, but the weight of that knowledge settled heavily upon their shoulders.

Theron took a deep breath, his voice steady despite the emotion welling in his throat. "We have to make the hard choices. It's the only way to ensure as many survive as possible."

Dorian placed a comforting hand on Theron's shoulder, his eyes filled with understanding. "You're right. But there may be another way." He turned to Callista, a flicker of hope in his gaze. "What about Akrotiri? It's further from the mountain, and there are bound to be more fishing boats and small vessels there. We did plan to sue it if necessary."

Callista considered the suggestion, her mind racing. It was a gamble, but one that could save lives. Their original plan had accounted for them having more time than she thought they had now. Aisforos was awakening much faster than she, or Theron, had thought possible. She nodded slowly, a plan forming in her mind. "We'll send those who can't fit here to Akrotiri. It's their best chance."

Theron jumped into action, his voice rising above the noise. "Everyone, listen! If you can't find a place on a ship here, head to Akrotiri! There will be more boats there, more chances for escape. Stick together, help each other."

A ripple of murmurs spread through the crowd, a mix of relief and trepidation. The elderly woman's face softened, tears of gratitude streaming down her weathered cheeks. "Thank you," she whispered, clutching her grandson's hand tightly.

Callista turned to Dorian and Theron, a fierce determination burning in her eyes. "We'll make this work. No one gets left behind, not if we can help it."

Dorian grinned, his optimism infectious despite the dire circumstances. "Together, we can achieve the impossible. Thera's people are strong, resilient. We'll weather this storm and rebuild."

As the trio set about organizing the remaining evacuees, directing them to the appropriate vessels or the road to Akrotiri, a sense of unity settled over the harbor. In the face of unimaginable adversity, the people of Thera were coming together, bound by hope and the unwavering belief in the strength of their community.

Captain Minoas stood at the helm of his ship, his weathered hand resting on the polished wood as he surveyed the organized chaos of the harbor. The first wave of ships bobbed gently in the water, their decks packed with anxious faces and hastily gathered belongings. Minoas caught the eye of his first mate, Demetrios, and nodded solemnly.

"It's time," Minoas called out, his deep voice cutting through the din of the crowd. "Cast off the lines and raise the sails. We've got precious cargo to deliver to safety."

As the crew sprang into action, Theron made his way through the throng of people still waiting on the docks. His heart ached for those who couldn't board the ships, their desperation palpable in the air. He climbed the gangplank of Minoas' vessel, his robes fluttering in the breeze.

"Captain Minoas," Theron said, his voice steady despite the weight of the moment. "For those who remain, I've advised them to make for Akrotiri. With luck, they'll find passage on the fishing boats and merchant ships there."

Minoas clasped Theron's shoulder, his grip firm and reassuring. "A wise plan, Brother Theron. We'll head to Akrotiri ourselves to ensure they're prepared for the influx of refugees. The triad from the Scroll of Aisforos should be coming with me."

Theron bounded back onto the dock to where Callista and Dorian waited. "No, we will evacuate the rest of the priestesses from the temple and head to Akrotiri. Meet us there Captain." Callista ordered. Captain Minoas nodded as he stole another glance up at the mountain. Callista, understanding his gaze said "The Mother will protect us, and you Captain. Go! With Potnia's blessings." The Captain stared into her eyes, the fear subsiding, and ordered his crew to make for Akrotiri.

Chapter 14: The Temple's Last Night

Callista's silhouette danced against the ancient walls as she stepped into the Temple of Potnia one last time. The hem of her robe whispered across the cool stone floors, a soft hush that seemed to murmur secrets of ages past. Dorian and Theron followed close behind, their presence like shadows tethered to her light.

"Smells like the heavens in here," Dorian remarked, his voice mingling with the heavy scent of incense that filled the air.

"Indeed," Callista replied, her tone laced with reverence. "The gods are generous with their blessings."

Theron glanced around, the flickering brazier light casting an otherworldly glow on his thoughtful face. "It's as if the very shadows are alive, whispering the goddess's wisdom," he said, more to himself than to the others.

"Perhaps they are," Callista said, smiling at his fascination. "Keep your senses open, and you might hear more than just whispers."

As they delved deeper into the heart of the temple, the outside world seemed to fade away, replaced by an enveloping serenity. Each step they took was purposeful, drawn by the pull of the sacred space ahead. Silence settled comfortably among them, the last of the priestesses had been evacuated to Akrotiri an hour earlier.

"Here we are," Callista announced softly as they approached the small underground inner sanctum. She paused before the entrance, her green eyes reflecting the calm certainty of her spirit. "The pool of Potnia awaits."

Dorian peered into the dimly lit chamber, his usual humor giving way to solemnity. "It looks... ancient," he whispered, as though afraid to disturb the quietude of the sanctum.

"Timeless, as the goddess herself," Callista corrected gently, leading them forward with a grace that seemed almost otherworldly. "If we are forced to abandon this place then I will bathe in the grace of the goddess one last time." Her ribbons and beads caught the sparse light, winking like stars caught in her dark tresses.

"Let us proceed with the respect such antiquity deserves," Theron added, his ink-stained fingers unconsciously reaching for his satchel, perhaps longing to record the moment.

Callista's fingers lingered on the edge of the ancient stone, her touch almost reverent as she and her companions beheld the pool's transformation. The waters, once reflective and still as glass, now sent up tendrils of steam that curled into the air like offerings to the heavens.

"By the breath of Potnia," Theron murmured, his scholarly eyes widening in awe, "the cold womb of earth has been warmed by her divine hand."

Dorian let out a low whistle, the sound somehow respectful within the hallowed space. "I've sailed the Aegean and seen wonders, but this..." He trailed off, shaking his head with a smile of disbelief. "This is a different kind of magic."

The warmth that radiated from the pool seemed to beckon them closer, an invisible embrace from the goddess herself. Callista nodded at the silent invitation, her movements calm and purposeful. Her fingers moved with deliberate grace as she reached for the sash at her waist, the soft fabric cool beneath her touch. With a calm and practiced motion, her hands unwound the luxurious silk, each twist releasing a subtle, shimmering cascade. The sash slipped away, whispering against her skin as it descended in a graceful arc, finally pooling like liquid moonlight on the cool, polished floor. In the past exposing her naked skin in this chamber resulted in a thrilling chill running through her, but the changes to the chamber from the warmed water and stone gave her a completely different sensation.

"Through this act, we leave behind all that binds us to the mundane," she declared, her voice resonating like a melodious thread woven through the sacred stillness of the sanctum. The dim light cast intricate shadows on the stone walls, flickering from the candles that lined the altar. Callista, her eyes shining with a serene intensity, turned to the two men standing before her. Dorian, with his dark hair falling over his forehead, glanced at Theron, whose steady gaze met Callista's. "Please, join me," she continued with a warm smile, extending her hand toward them both, inviting them to disrobe and enter the pool.

Dorian followed her example, his movements more practical than ceremonial, but no less sincere. His garments joined Callista's on the stone, a patchwork of colors against the grey. A grin tugged at the corner of his mouth as he glanced at Theron. "Your turn, my friend. Don't worry, the goddess appreciates scholars in their natural state too."

Theron's cheeks colored, a rare sight for the man usually so composed in his thoughts. With a sheepish nod, he disrobed, folding his simple robes with methodical care before placing them beside the others'. His gaze was drawn to the steaming waters, anticipation clear in his thoughtful eyes.

"May we be as unburdened as we are unclothed," Theron intoned, his words carrying the weight of belief and curiosity.

"May our spirits be as light as our bodies," Callista continued, leading them to the edge of the pool with a look of serenity that seemed to illuminate the chamber.

"May our laughter be as free as our hearts," Dorian added, his smile warm and unabashed as he completed the impromptu litany.

Together, they stood at the water's edge, the warmth caressing their skin, and the scent of incense and herbs wrapping around them—a tapestry of sensation that promised both solace and revelation. They were poised on the cusp of the sacred, ready to immerse themselves in the mysteries of Potnia, their bond a trifecta of strength, wisdom, and courage.

The step into the steaming waters was like crossing into another realm. Callista led the way, her body reacting with a slight shiver as the warmth of the bath wrapped around her. Dorian followed, a low chuckle escaping him as he surrendered to the liquid heat, his eyes closing for a moment in appreciation. Theron, ever the observer, hesitated just a second before easing himself into the pool, his analytical mind cataloging the sensation even as his muscles relaxed.

"Ah, to think the sea would envy this warmth," Dorian murmured, his voice a soft rumble.

"Indeed," Callista agreed, allowing herself a rare, small smile at Dorian's comment. Her gaze then settled on the ripples they had created, watching them spread and fade into stillness.

"Potnia, Mother of Earth, Sea, and Sky," she began, her voice barely louder than the whisper of steam rising from the water. "We seek your protection as we enter these sacred depths."

Dorian glanced over at Theron, who nodded solemnly, his brown eyes reflecting the flickering light from nearby braziers. Together, they fixed their attention on Callista, recognizing the gravity of her words within the embrace of Potnia's temple.

"Guide our hearts and minds," Callista continued, her prayer flowing with the same natural grace as the tendrils of warmth that curled through the water. "Grant us clarity to see beyond the veil of the material, to the essence that binds us all."

"Guide our hearts and minds," Dorian echoed softly, and Theron repeated the invocation in his precise, thoughtful manner.

"Let our union be blessed by your divine hand, that we may serve you with love and wisdom." Callista's eyes closed briefly, her lips moving in silent supplication.

A hush fell over the trio, the only sounds the gentle lapping of water against stone and the distant, melodic chanting of priestesses far above. The scent of incense wove through the air, mingling with the earthy aroma of the oils soon to anoint their skin.

"May it be so," Theron said, his analytical mind yielding to the ancient ritual that felt more real and potent than any theory or observation.

"May it be so," Dorian agreed, smiling at the shared reverence of the moment. His usual jovial demeanor was tempered by awe, the humor in his eyes replaced by a depth of emotion.

Callista opened her eyes, and in the dim light of the chamber, they seemed to glow with an inner fire. She gave a nod of approval, satisfied with their united front—a triad of trust in the divine and in each other. They were ready to proceed, their bodies and spirits cleansed and prepared for what was to come.

With the incantations lingering like whispers against the chamber walls, Callista reached for the alabaster jar cradled near the pool's edge. The sacred olive oil within was as much a part of the ritual as the water that had embraced them moments before. She uncorked it delicately, allowing the aroma to rise and blend with the steam—a fragrance of earth and divinity.

"May our intentions be as pure as this offering," she murmured, tilting the jar to pour the oil onto her palm. It shimmered like liquid gold against her skin, anointing her hand with its sanctity.

Dorian watched, his smile subdued by the gravity of the moment. His chest rose with a breath of appreciation, not just for the scent but also for the symbolism. "As clear as our purpose," he replied, accepting the vessel when she offered it to him.

Callista turned first to Dorian, her fingers dancing across his shoulders, trailing lines of oil in patterns that spoke of protection and strength. Her touch was light, the reverence in her movements telling more than words ever could. Each curve and stroke was an unspoken prayer, a silent vow of her commitment to their shared path.

"Potnia watches over us," she said softly, her voice blending seamlessly with the gentle sounds of the sanctuary.

Dorian nodded, the warmth of her touch igniting something deeper within him. When it was his turn, he poured the oil into his own palms with care, watching it glisten against the rugged terrain of his sailor's hands. He met her gaze, his eyes alight with a brilliant mix of respect and affection.

"May our bond be as strong as the sea," Dorian intoned, hands coming to rest upon Callista's arms. His fingers moved with a sailor's deftness, weaving a narrative of trust and companionship upon her skin. Though his life was one of winds and waves, this connection, here on solid ground, felt like anchoring in a safe harbor.

Her skin caught the flickering brazier light as if she herself were a beacon. "And as enduring," she responded, a soft chuckle escaping her. It was rare for her to show such lightheartedness during a ceremony—yet here, now, it felt right.

"May we navigate this journey together," Dorian added, his tone carrying the cadence of an oath as solemn as any he'd uttered under open skies.

"Under her watchful eye," Callista finished, her eyes reflecting the flames' dance, her heart warmed by the honesty in Dorian's voice. Together, they were two points of a sacred triangle, united in purpose and enveloped in the tender grace of their goddess.

Theron took the slender phial of oil from Callista's outstretched hand, his fingertips lightly brushing hers in a silent thanks. He unscrewed the cap methodically, as if each turn of his wrist was a calculated step in an elaborate equation. The oil's aroma rose to greet him—a blend of herbs and earth that seemed to whisper secrets of the island itself.

"Precision is a form of prayer, wouldn't you say?" Theron mused aloud, his voice a tranquil note against the backdrop of the sanctum's quietude. He nodded to himself, affirming his own words before turning to face Dorian.

"Absolutely," Dorian agreed with a grin, "though I've always found the sea to be more forgiving than numbers."

"Then let us hope Potnia appreciates both," Callista added, her eyes shimmering with a gentle humor that echoed the warmth of the chamber.

Theron's hands were steady, a testament to the countless hours spent charting stars and scribbling observations. He dipped his fingers in the oil, coating them with a sheen that caught the light. With a touch that married tenderness and assurance, he traced a sigil upon Dorian's forehead—one that spoke of protection and wisdom.

"May clarity guide your journey," Theron intoned solemnly, his thumb pausing on the center of Dorian's brow.

"Clarity and a good tailwind," Dorian chuckled, closing his eyes to savor the coolness of the oil against his skin.

Next, Theron turned to Callista. He hesitated for a moment, his gaze lingering on the ribbons in her hair, the way they seemed like threads of fate woven through the tapestry of her dark curls. Then, with a reverence befitting the High Priestess, he anointed her shoulders in a crisscross pattern, drawing lines as if mapping constellations on her flesh.

"May your spirit be as boundless as the sky above," he whispered, and Callista's lips curved into a soft smile, acknowledging the depth behind his words.

"Boundless and serene," she replied, returning the warmth of his gesture with a glance filled with gratitude.

With their bodies adorned in the sacred oil and their spirits interlaced with the devotion of their actions, the three companions stepped back, inhaling the mingled scents of olive and incense that enveloped them like an ethereal cloak. They turned to face the altar on the edge of the ancient pool, its stone surface was hewn from the rock of the chamber itself, etched with eons of offerings.

"Shall we?" Dorian asked, extending a hand to each of his companions.

"Let's," Callista affirmed, taking his hand in hers while Theron clasped the other.

Their movements mirrored one another as they approached the altar, their steps measured and deliberate. The rhythm of their footfalls harmonized with the distant murmur of priestess chants, creating a symphony of purpose that resonated through the sanctum's walls.

"Here we stand, together," Callista said, her voice a soft but firm declaration as they halted before the altar.

"United in heart and intent," Theron continued, his analytical gaze softening with emotion.

"Ready to honor the Great Mother," Dorian finished, his warm smile a beacon of shared conviction.

And there, in the embrace of the Temple of Potnia, they stood as one—a triad of earth, sea, and sky, ready to merge their individual strengths into a singular offering of devotion.

Gently, as if the very air of the temple urged them to caution, Callista, Dorian, and Theron arranged themselves upon the time-worn altar. The coolness of the stone beneath contrasted with the warmth of their skin from the pool, slick with the olive oil, anointed and fragrant.

Callista's slender fingers found their way to Dorian's length, stroking him gently as her eyes locked onto his. Theron watched intently while his hands explored Callista's body. He cupped her breasts tenderly and brushed his fingertips across her hardened nipples. The sensation sent shivers down her spine as she arched her back in response.

Dorian leaned in to claim Callista's lips with his own as Theron pressed himself against her from behind. A moan escaped her lips when she felt Theron's throbbing erection push against her lower back. Her body responded eagerly as she welcomed the simultaneous sensations of both men touching her.

The trio shifted, and Callista positioned herself on all fours, inviting Dorian to enter her from the front. He obliged, gently guiding his slickened member into her warm depths, while Theron took the opportunity to slide into her from behind. The dual penetration sent waves of ecstasy coursing through Callista's body, and her moans filled the chamber.

Their bodies moved together in a sensual rhythm, guided by devotion and desire. Each thrust brought them closer to their peak, but they held back, savoring every moment and every touch. Finally, with a shared understanding of their intent, they allowed themselves to let go.

As one, they climaxed—earth, sea, and sky united in a display of pleasure that echoed through the Temple of Potnia. But that was not the end.

Callista positioned herself above Dorian, kneeling above his head, inviting his mouth to her. Callista straddled Dorian's face, guiding his eager mouth to her glistening folds. He licked and sucked at her sensitive nub as she moaned above him. Theron parted Dorian's legs and rubbed his oiled legs before easing into Dorian's previously untouched area. Waves of pleasure intermingled with an unfamiliar sensation washed over Dorian as he welcomed this new experience with open arms and a lustful heart. The pressure he felt gave way slowly, and he gasped in previously unfelt pleasures.

Callista's wetness coated Dorian's lips and he eagerly licked and sucked at her most sensitive areas. Callista moaned above him, her body trembling with pleasure as she rocked her hips against his mouth. She could feel the energy building within her, ready to burst into a powerful release.

Theron continued to work his magic, causing Dorian to gasp in previously unfelt pleasures. His mind raced as waves of intense pleasure rippled through him, each one more powerful than the last with each thrust from Theron. Dorian found himself lost in ecstasy as Callista ground herself on his face and Theron brought him closer and closer to a peak he had never experienced before. As they moved together in perfect harmony, their bodies seemed to merge into one—earth, sea, and sky united once again.

Finally, with a shared cry of release, they came together again for the second time—three individual energies combining into one powerful force. Callista collapsed onto Dorian's chest while Theron lay between them, panting heavily.

For a few moments, they simply lay there in silent bliss before slowly untangling themselves from each other's embrace. As they sat up and began gathering their clothes scattered around them on the altar, a sense of fulfillment washed over them.

They had honored the Great Mother in a way that only a triad of earth, sea, and sky could. In the aftermath of their fervent offering, the temple's inner sanctum held a sacred hush. Callista moved and nestled between Dorian and Theron, her breaths syncing with theirs in a rhythm as old as time. The warmth of the bath seeped into their bones, the lingering fragrance of olive oil a testament to the ritual they had just performed.

"Feels like we've been touched by the divine," murmured Dorian, his voice a soft thread in the quietude.

"Or perhaps we've simply remembered what it is to be truly alive," Theron suggested, his analytical mind never far from contemplation, even in moments of profound stillness.

Callista's eyelids fluttered open, her gaze holding each of them in turn. "Both, I think," she said, her voice imbued with the serenity that came from fulfilling one's purpose. "We are renewed, not just by Potnia's grace, but by the strength we give each other."

They remained thus for several heartbeats, the gentle embrace a cocoon against the world outside. But as all moments do, this one too whispered towards its end. With a collective sigh that seemed to echo off the ancient stones, they untangled themselves and rose from the altar.

"Shall we?" Callista extended her hands, palms open and inviting. Dorian and Theron accepted the gesture, their hands clasping hers in an unspoken vow of unity.

"Back to the warmth we go," Dorian said with a chuckle, leading them back to the steaming pool that promised comfort after the intensity of their shared experience.

"Like moths to a flame," Theron added, the hint of a smile on his lips suggesting he wasn't entirely immune to Dorian's infectious humor.

One by one, they stepped down into the hot waters, sighing in unison as the heat welcomed them back. They settled into the liquid embrace, the ripples of the pool lapping gently at their skin, echoing the tranquility that now filled their hearts.

"Here we are, reborn," Callista spoke softly, her green eyes reflecting the flickering light from the braziers. "Not just in flesh, but in spirit."

"Reborn, and ready for whatever comes next," Dorian agreed, his hand finding Callista's beneath the water, a silent affirmation of their connection.

"Indeed," Theron concurred, his analytical gaze softened by the camaraderie that bound them. "United, as we must always be."

The steam curled around them like a benevolent spirit, and for a long moment, they simply existed together, their laughter and whispers becoming part of the temple's eternal song.

Chapter 15: Betrayal in Akrotiri

The salty sea breeze whipped Callista's hair across her face as she stepped onto the crowded streets of Akrotiri. Beside her, Dorian and Theron exchanged tense glances, their eyes darting warily over the throngs of people jostling to board the waiting ships. The distant rumble of the volcano thundered in their ears, an ominous reminder of the urgency of their mission.

"By the gods, it's chaos here," Dorian muttered, sidestepping a cart piled high with belongings. "We'll be lucky to make it to the temple in one piece."

Callista nodded grimly, her hand tightening on the sacred amulet at her throat. The panicked cries of children and the frantic bellows of men loading provisions onto the ships down by the docks tore at her heart. She knew all too well the fear that gripped them.

As they wove their way through the narrow streets, the tang of smoke began to mingle with the scent of the sea. Ahead, the white stone walls of the temple loomed, a beacon of hope in the pandemonium. But Callista's steps faltered as she spotted a cluster of grim-faced men in robes that marked them as members of the Priest-Kings acolytes, his cultists.

"This doesn't bode well," Theron said quietly, his brow furrowed.

Callista met his gaze, seeing her own worry reflected there. "Lykos," she said simply. "His influence reaches even here."

Dorian's jaw clenched. "Then we'll just have to reach further. Ariadne needs us."

With a deep breath, Callista squared her shoulders and strode forward, Dorian and Theron flanking her. As they approached, the hard eyes of the authorities turned toward them, their expressions as unyielding as the stone beneath their feet.

Callista's heart hammered in her chest, but she kept her voice steady as she inclined her head in greeting. "Gentlemen. I am Callista

Antheia, High Priestess of the Cult of Potnia. I urgently seek an audience within the temple."

The men exchanged glances, their coldness palpable. "The temple is occupied with vital matters of state," one said brusquely. "They have no time for outsiders and their groundless fearmongering."

Callista bristled at the accusation, but before she could respond, Dorian stepped forward, his manner all easy charm. "Surely, in times of crisis, the wisdom of the Temple priests is needed more than ever. We only wish to offer what aid and guidance we can, in service to your people. What can we do to sway you to arrange an audience?" A wink and a glint accompanied his words.

As the men conferred in low voices, Callista shot Dorian a grateful look. His silver tongue and disarming nature had eased many a tense negotiation over the years. Perhaps, with the gods' blessing, this would be no exception. She cast her gaze imploringly up at the smoke-streaked sky. Potnia, Great Mother, guide our steps. The fate of Thera hangs in the balance.

The senior sycophant of the Priest-King emerged from the hushed conference, his expression severe. "We will not grant you an audience in the temple," he declared, his voice dripping with disdain. "However, I have a message for you. Your priestess, Ariadne, has been detained for spreading your seditious lies. She will face the consequences of her actions."

Callista's blood ran cold. Ariadne, sweet, impulsive Ariadne, locked away for her loyalty. She exchanged a stricken glance with Theron, whose jaw tightened with barely suppressed anger. "I demand to see her," Callista said, her voice low and fierce. "As High Priestess, it is my right to oversee the welfare of my charges."

The cultist's lip curled. "You presume much, outsider. The temple of Akrotiri falls under the authority of the priest-king, not cult of the mother."

Callista drew herself up to her full height, her green eyes flashing. "The Cult of Potnia is the preeminent religious authority on Thera. Our rites and mysteries predate the priest-king's rule. I will not ask again. Take me to Ariadne."

For a long moment, the sycophant held her gaze, a silent battle of wills. Then, with a curt nod, he turned on his heel. "Follow me."

They descended into the bowels of the temple, the air growing colder and damper with each step. The only light came from the flickering torch in the priest's hand, casting distorted shadows on the rough-hewn walls.

At last, they reached a heavy wooden door, which the priest unlocked with a large, rusty key. "You have a quarter of an hour," he said, his tone making it clear that he would grant no more.

Callista nodded, her heart in her throat, and stepped into the cell. There, in the dim light, sat Ariadne, her white acolyte's robes smudged with grime and blood, her curly red hair tangled and matted. But when she raised her head, her eyes sparkled with unquenchable spirit.

"High Priestess," she breathed, her voice trembling with emotion. "I knew you would come."

Callista crossed the cell in two strides and gathered the girl into her arms, feeling the frantic beat of her heart. "Oh, Ariadne," she murmured, her own eyes stinging with unshed tears. "What have they done to you?"

Ariadne clung to her, her slight frame shaking with a mix of fear and relief. "They questioned me for hours," she whispered. "They wanted me to recant, to say that your visions were false. But I couldn't. I wouldn't."

Callista's heart swelled with pride and sorrow. This brave, foolish girl, willing to endure such hardship for her faith. "You have been so strong, Ariadne. But I promise you, we will find a way to set this right. The Mother will not abandon us."

As she held Ariadne close, Callista's mind raced. They had to free her, but how? And how could they hope to evacuate a town that is in such chaos? The weight of her task seemed to press down on her, as heavy and inexorable as the mountain that loomed over them all. But she was the High Priestess. She could not falter now. For Ariadne, for all of Thera, she had to find a way. May Potnia guide her steps, for she would need all the divine aid she could muster in the trials to come.

Theron stepped forward, his usually gentle face hardened with determination. "We won't leave you here, Ariadne," he said firmly. "I don't care what Lykos or his cultists says. You're one of us, and we protect our own."

Dorian nodded, his warm eyes glinting with a new steely resolve. "Theron's right. We'll find a way to get you out of here, even if we have to break down the door ourselves."

Ariadne managed a watery smile, her spirits lifting at their unwavering support. "I knew you wouldn't abandon me," she said softly. "But how will we convince the Lykos and his cult? They're so set against us now."

Callista released Ariadne, stepping back to look at her companions. The dimly lit cell seemed to close in around them, a physical manifestation of the obstacles they faced. But in the determined faces of her friends, she found a glimmer of hope.

"We'll have to be clever," she said thoughtfully. "Lykos has turned many against us, and most of those from the capital who believed in us are gone on ships, but there are still those who might listen."

Theron's eyes lit up. "The tremors," he said excitedly. "I've been tracking them, and they're growing more frequent. If we can show the cultists my records, maybe they'll see the pattern."

Dorian clapped him on the shoulder. "That's brilliant, Theron! And I have contacts in the harbor, people who've seen the changes in the sea. If we pool our knowledge, surely we can make them understand. As long as we can speak to them without Lykos being around..."

Callista felt a flicker of pride. Her little flock, so brave and resourceful. Perhaps, with Potnia's blessing, they could yet save their people. "Then that's what we'll do," she said, her voice ringing with newfound conviction. "Theron, gather your records. Dorian, speak to your contacts. We'll present our case to the cultists, and pray that they see reason."

She turned back to Ariadne, clasping her hands. "And you, my dear, must be our eyes and ears here. Listen to the guards, to the priests. Any whisper, any hint of a change in the winds, could be vital."

Ariadne straightened, her tears drying as purpose filled her. "I won't let you down, Callista. I'll be strong, for all of us."

As they made their plans, whispering urgently in the flickering torchlight, Callista felt the first stirrings of real hope. It would not be easy, she knew. Lykos's influence ran deep, and fear was a powerful enemy. But they had truth on their side, and the blessings of the Mother.

***

Callista strode through the arched doorway of the Temple in Akrotiri, her sandals echoing on the polished stone. The gathered cultists fell silent as she entered, their eyes tracking her every move. Suspicion hung thick in the air, mingling with the scent of olive oil lamps and incense.

At the head of the room, Lykos lounged on an elevated chair, his expression a mask of disdain. "Callista Antheia," he drawled, his voice dripping with condescension. "To what do we owe this... unexpected pleasure?"

Callista met his gaze unflinchingly, her chin held high. She had hoped to address his followers without his presence, this was an unwelcome surprise. "I come bearing urgent news, Lykos. News that concerns the very survival of our people."

Her words failed to stir the sycophants around the Priest-King, Lykos merely smiled, a cold, reptilian thing. "Ah, yes. Your prophecies of doom. Tell me, Callista, do you truly expect us to heed the ravings of a failed priestess?"

Callista felt anger flare within her, hot and bright, but she tamped it down. Losing her temper would only play into Lykos's hands. Instead, she turned to address the council as a whole, her voice calm and clear. "Esteemed citizens of Thera, I come to you not as a priestess, but as a daughter of Thera. Like you, I have sworn to protect and serve our people. And like you, I cannot ignore the signs that our island is in grave danger."

She reached into her satchel, withdrawing a sheaf of papyrus scrolls. "I have here records from our fishermen, our farmers, our sailors. All telling the same story: the mountain grows restless. The earth trembles. The sea boils. We cannot afford to turn a blind eye."

Lykos scoffed, waving a dismissive hand. "Fairy tales and old wives' tales. Hardly evidence of impending disaster."

But some of his cultists were leaning forward, curiosity and concern warring on their faces. Callista pressed her advantage, her voice growing more impassioned.

"Is it a fairy tale that our crops withered in the fields? That our fish float belly-up in the harbor? That the very ground beneath our feet shudders and cracks?" She shook her head, her eyes blazing. "No, my friends. This is the warning of the Mother herself. And if we do not heed it, we will all perish."

The chamber erupted into a cacophony of voices, some angry, some afraid, some simply confused. Lykos's face had gone red with fury, his fists clenched at his sides. But Callista stood tall amidst the chaos, her faith unwavering.

"Please," she implored, her voice rising above the din. "I ask only that you listen. That you examine the evidence with open minds and open hearts. Your lives hang in the balance. Already most of our people are gone in ships, destined for a new home. Do not be left behind." Callista caught Lykos's eye across the room. In that moment, she saw the depth of his hatred, the lengths to which he would go to silence her. But she also saw something else, something that sent a chill down her spine.

Fear. Lykos was afraid. Afraid of her, afraid of the truth, afraid of losing his grip on power. And that, Callista realized, made him more dangerous than the triad had thought.

***

The lock on Ariadne's cell door clicked open, and Dorian eased it open, his heart pounding in his chest. Theron stood watch at the end of the corridor, his eyes darting nervously from side to side.

"Ariadne," Dorian whispered, slipping into the cell. "It's us."

The young priestess leapt to her feet, her eyes wide with relief. "Dorian! Theron! Thank the Mother you're here."

"Shh," Dorian cautioned, pressing a finger to his lips. "We've got to be quick and quiet. Callista's buying us time with Lykos' cultists, but we don't know how long she can hold them off."

Ariadne nodded, her face set with determination. "I'm ready."

Theron glanced over his shoulder, his voice low and urgent. "We need to hurry. The guards could return at any moment."

Dorian took Ariadne's hand, his grip warm and reassuring. "Stay close to me. Theron will lead the way."

Together, they slipped out of the cell, their footsteps echoing softly on the stone floor. Theron guided them through the labyrinthine corridors, his knowledge of the temple's layout proving invaluable.

As they moved, Dorian leaned close to Ariadne, his voice a comforting murmur. "It's going to be alright. We'll get you out of here, I promise."

Ariadne squeezed his hand, her eyes shining with gratitude. "I knew you would come for me. I never lost faith."

***

In the upper temple chambers, Callista stood firm against the onslaught of questions and accusations, her voice clear and unwavering.

"You speak of chaos and fear," one cultist challenged, his face twisted with anger. "But it is you who brings these things to our people!"

Callista met his gaze, her expression serene. "I speak only the truth, honored councilman. The signs are clear for those with eyes to see."

"Signs?" another scoffed. "What signs? The ravings of a mad priestess?"

"The earth trembles beneath our feet," Callista replied, her voice soft but insistent. "The mountain spews fire and ash. The Mother sends us warnings, if only we would heed them."

A murmur rippled through the chamber, and Callista saw a flicker of doubt in some of their eyes. She pressed on, her words measured and calm. "I understand your fears, your doubts. But I ask you to look beyond them, to the welfare of yourselves and your families. We must act now, before it is too late to get you off the island."

Just as the Lykos opened his mouth to retort, a violent tremor shook the building, sending a shower of dust and debris raining down from the ceiling. Callista braced herself against a marble pillar, her heart pounding as the ground beneath her feet seemed to come alive.

Screams of terror filled the chamber as the councilors clung to their seats, their faces pale with fear. In the chaos, Callista's voice rang out clear and strong. "Do you see now?" she cried, her eyes blazing with conviction. "The Mother speaks to us, even in this moment!"

***

Deep within the temple's labyrinthine corridors, Dorian and Theron felt the tremor's power. Dust rained down from the ancient stone walls, and the ground beneath their feet seemed to heave and buckle.

"Hurry!" Theron hissed, his voice tight with urgency. "The guards will be distracted. This is our chance!"

Together, the trio raced through the twisting passageways, their footsteps echoing off the stone walls. With each turn, Dorian's heart pounded faster, the thrill of their escape tempered by the knowledge of the danger that still lurked outside the temple walls. But as they burst into the open air, the sun warm on their faces, he couldn't help but feel a sense of victory.

They had done it. Ariadne was free, and together, they would face whatever challenges lay ahead. But first, they had a people to lead to safety. Dorian turned to his companions. "Let's find Callista," he said, his voice ringing with purpose. "Together, we will make sure your people survive this crisis."

As Callista emerged from the Temple, her heart racing with the urgency of their situation, she spotted Dorian, Theron, and Ariadne hurrying towards her. Relief flooded through her at the sight of Ariadne's newfound freedom, a testament to the courage and loyalty of her companions.

"Thank the gods you're safe," Callista breathed, embracing Ariadne warmly. She turned to Dorian and Theron, her eyes shining with gratitude. "And thank you both for your bravery. I knew I could count on you."

Theron grinned, his usual bravado tempered by the gravity of their circumstances. "We couldn't leave our favorite priestess behind, now could we?"

Dorian, his hand resting lightly on Callista's arm, met her gaze with a mixture of concern and determination. "How did it go with the cultists? Were you able to convince them?"

Callista sighed, the weight of her responsibilities settling heavily on her shoulders. "Some were swayed, but others remain firmly under Lykos's influence. Once the Priest King made it clear he didn't believe me, and he was staying on Thera, they all joined with him. I failed to save any of them."

Ariadne, her eyes brimming with tears said. "The people trust you, Callista, but not everyone can be saved, sometimes we cannot save people from themselves."

Dorian nodded in agreement, "I have seen this before, a leader with such a devoted group of followers that no matter what anyone else says, nor how much the leader lies, they will not abandon the leader."

But even as she understood they were right, her mind was consumed by thoughts of Lykos and the depth of his betrayal. How could a man who had once been her mentor, her guide in the ways of the priesthood, turn so coldly against her? Against the very people he had sworn to protect?

As they approached the central square, the heart of Akrotiri, Callista could see the crowds beginning to gather. Merchants and fishermen, mothers and children, all drawn in the desperate hope for guidance.

Callista ascended the steps of the central fountain, her heart pounding in her chest as she turned to face the sea of faces before her. The murmurs of the crowd quieted as she raised her hands, the sacred beads on her wrists catching the sunlight.

"People of Akrotiri," she began, her voice ringing out clear and strong. "I come to you today not just as your High Priestess, but as a fellow child of Thera. One who has seen the signs of the Great Mother's warning, and who fears for the safety of our beloved home. It is true, we have already evacuated our capital, many of those who could not fit on our ships made their way here over land to board whatever ships you have to spare. We are all Therans here, we serve Potnia, and she calls on us to help each other!"

She could see the fear in their eyes, the uncertainty that rippled through the crowd. But there was something else there too, a flicker of hope, a desperate longing for guidance.

Dorian stepped forward, his presence a comforting strength at her side. "We have all heard the rumors," he said, his voice carrying the cadence of a storyteller. "Lykos..." a gasp rippled through the crowd at the use of the name without a title before it, "Is lost to you. He will not help you, he will not lead you to safety. Following him will be like march to the shores of the river Styx!"

Ariadne, her red curls gleaming in the sunlight, spoke next, her words tumbling out in an eager rush. "I have seen it, I have felt it!" She held up her arms so the assembled Therans could see her dirty, bloddy, tattered robes. Once the pristine white of her order. "The colors of my sacred order have been defiled by Lykos' sycophantic cultists! They match the crimes committed against me as a daughter of Potnia!" The crowd grew angry at the thought of one of their priestesses being treated so badly.

Theron, his ink-stained fingers clutching a sheaf of notes, stepped forward to join them. "I have studied the ancient texts of Thera, we as a people have weathered storms before and remained whole, though we travel to distant shores, we will remain Therans!"

The crowd stirred, a rising tide of fear and confusion. Callista could feel their terror, could see the way they clung to each other, desperate for answers.

"There is hope," she cried, her voice rising above the din. "Potnia has shown us the way, has given us the chance to save ourselves and all that we hold dear. Make room in your hearts, on your ships, and in your fishing boats for all Therans who wish to escape."

Chapter 16: The Awakening

Callista stood amid the chaos engulfing Akrotiri, her heart pounding in rhythm with the trembling ground beneath her sandaled feet. Ash rained down from the sky, coating the once-pristine streets in a ghostly gray pallor. The air was thick with the acrid stench of sulfur, and the distant rumble of the awakening volcano droned ominously, an unrelenting reminder of the accuracy of her prophecies. A reminder of her home's doom.

All around her, panicked citizens raced through the streets, their faces etched with abject terror. Some clutched meager belongings, others clung desperately to wailing children. The cacophony of their cries mingled with the crash of pottery shattering as it fell from trembling shelves.

Callista's mind raced, seeking divine guidance to navigate this unprecedented crisis. She closed her eyes, blocking out the turmoil, and reached out to Potnia with every fiber of her being. "Great goddess, bestow your wisdom upon me in our hour of need," she whispered.

Callista turned, her gaze searching the chaos until it landed on the familiar faces of her companions. Dorian stood tall, his brow furrowed as he surveyed the panicked crowds. Theron's fingers twitched as if itching to record the unfolding disaster. Ariadne, her red curls escaping her temple veil, looked to Callista with wide, worried eyes.

She gathered them to her, raising her voice to be heard above the din. "The Scroll of Aisforos and the paintings in the sacred cave showed us what's to come. The volcano will erupt with a fury unlike anything we've ever seen. Thera will be consumed by fire and waves. By ash and tides!"

Ariadne gasped, her hands flying to her mouth. "By the gods! What can we do?"

Callista gripped the young acolyte's shoulder, her voice steady despite the urgency thrumming through her veins. "We must act swiftly to save as many lives as possible. I fear it may already be too late." She stole a glance upward, where the mountain should have been, but thick black ash hid it from her sight.

Theron nodded, his analytical mind already whirring. "If we coordinate our efforts, we can maximize the number of people we can get to safety."

Dorian's brow furrowed as he considered the logistics of trying to finish the evacuation of Akrotiri. "We'll need to organize the ships, ensure there's enough space for everyone." His eyes met Callista's, a glimmer of his usual warmth shining through the worry. "I can handle that, with the help of the other sailors. We'll make sure no one is left behind."

Callista nodded, grateful for Dorian's practical expertise. She turned to Theron, whose analytical gaze was fixed on the distant volcano. "Theron, what do you make of this? How much time do we have?"

"It's difficult to say with certainty, but based on the intensity of the tremors..." Theron paused, calculating. "We may have a matter of hours, a day at most, before the eruption reaches its peak."

Callista's heart clenched at the confirmation of the urgency she had gleaned from The Scroll of Aisforos. "Then we must move quickly. Dorian, gather the sailors and start preparing the ships. Theron, I need you to help spread the word, make sure everyone understands the gravity of the situation."

Theron nodded, his expression grave. "Of course, but Callista..." He hesitated, his eyes searching hers. "Be careful Callista." He embraced her in a strong hug and turned to leave before Callista could say anything.

Dorian approached her, he put his hand to the back of her head and pulled her into a passionate kiss. "We will see each other again. On a ship, or on the shores off Cyprus. I promise." He murmured in her ear.

As Dorian and Theron hurried off to their tasks, Callista looked after them, tears in her eyes. Hoping the triad was not breaking apart, never to reform again.

Ariadne stepped forward, her youthful face a mix of fear and determination. She placed a hand on her shoulder. "High Priestess, let me help rally the fishing community. They know me, they trust me. I can make sure they understand the danger and get them to the docks quickly."

Callista smiled at her young acolyte, her enthusiasm a welcome light amidst the darkness. "Thank you, Ariadne. Your connection to the fishing families will be invaluable. Gather them at the harbor, and help the elderly and children board the ships first."

Ariadne nodded, her red curls bouncing beneath her veil. "I won't let you down, High Priestess. Potnia guide us all." With a quick bow, she darted off towards the fishermen's quarter, her white robes still bloody and soiled from her imprisonment at the hands of Lykos' cultists fluttering in the ash-laden wind.

Callista watched her go, a flicker of hope in her heart. Despite her youth, Ariadne's bravery and love for her people shone through, a testament to the strength of the Theran spirit.

But there was no time to dwell on such thoughts. Callista turned her attention to the chaos around her, the screams and prayers of the frightened populace ringing in her ears. She moved through the crowd with purpose, her voice rising above the din.

"People of Akrotiri, hear me! By the grace of Potnia, we have been warned of the impending danger. We must make for the ships, quickly and calmly. Help your neighbors, carry only what is necessary. The temple guard will guide you to the harbor. May the Great Mother protect us all!"

Her words seemed to have an effect, the panic subsiding slightly as people began to move with more purpose toward the docks. Callista felt the weight of her responsibility settling on her shoulders, but she pushed forward, determined to see her people to safety.

As she made her way through the streets, she caught sight of Dorian and Theron, who were already hard at work organizing the evacuation. Dorian's booming voice carried over the crowd as he directed sailors and passengers alike, while Theron's calm presence helped soothe the frightened and uncertain.

Callista allowed herself a moment of gratitude for their presence, skills, and loyalty, a balm to her troubled soul. Together, they would face this trial, and with Potnia's blessing, they would overcome it.

Callista's sandals slapped against the cobblestone streets as she ran, her lungs burning with the effort. The air was thick with ash and the acrid scent of sulfur, a choking miasma that seared her throat with every breath. Around her, the people of Akrotiri fled in panic, their screams and cries blending into a cacophony of terror.

"To the docks!" Callista shouted, her voice raw and hoarse. "Everyone, head to the docks! The ships are waiting!"

She grabbed the arm of a stumbling old man, steadying him as she pushed him towards the harbor. "Quickly, father," she urged. "There's no time to waste."

The man nodded, his eyes wide with fear, and hurried on. Callista watched him go, her heart aching for the suffering of her people. But there was no time for sorrow, not now. She had to keep moving and guiding them to safety. A woman clutching a wailing infant caught her eye, and Callista rushed to her side. "Follow the others," she instructed, pointing towards the growing crowd heading for the docks. "The ships will take you to safety."

The woman nodded, tears streaking through the ash on her face. "Thank you, High Priestess," she whispered before hurrying away. Callista watched her go, a flicker of hope sparking in her chest. They could do this. They could save their people with Potnia's guidance and their own determination. But even as the thought crossed her mind, the ground heaved beneath her feet, sending her stumbling to her knees. A deafening roar filled the air, and Callista looked up to see a plume of smoke and fire erupting from the mountaintop, staining the sky an ominous red even through the dark haze of the ash.

With renewed urgency, Callista pushed forward, her voice rising above the din as she called out to her fleeing people. "Hurry! To the docks, everyone! We must leave now!"

***

Dorian's voice cut through the chaos, strong and reassuring. "People of Akrotiri, listen to me!" He stood atop a fallen pillar, his broad shoulders squared against the raining ash. "We have ships waiting at the docks. Follow the High Priestess, and we will guide you to safety!"

His words seemed to take hold, the panic in the air shifting to a fragile hope. A young boy, tears cutting through the grime on his face, tugged at Dorian's robes. "Will the ships take us away from the angry mountain?"

Dorian knelt, meeting the child's gaze with a gentle smile. "Yes, little one. The ships will carry you to a new home, where the ground does not shake, and the air is sweet." He ruffled the boy's hair, then stood, pointing towards the harbor. "Now, hurry along with your family. The High Priestess will make sure you're safe."

As the child scampered off, Dorian turned to Callista, his eyes reflecting the determination in her own. "We're making progress, but we need to move faster. The eruption grows closer by the moment."

Callista nodded, her gaze sweeping over the chaotic streets. "Theron, you know these alleys better than anyone. Can you find us a quicker path to the docks?"

The young priest stepped forward, his brow furrowed in thought. "There's a series of side streets that wind behind our small agora. They're narrow, but they should be less crowded." He hesitated, a flicker of worry in his eyes. "But, High Priestess, what if we can't get everyone to the ships in time?"

Callista laid a hand on his shoulder, her voice firm but compassionate. "We must trust in Potnia's guidance, Theron. She has shown me the path, and we will follow it, no matter the obstacles." She turned to the others, her chin lifted in resolve. "Lead the way, Theron. We'll make sure our people are right behind you."

***

Ariadne darted through the crowd, her red curls bouncing with each step. She paused to help a young boy who had stumbled, his hand clutching a small wooden horse. "Come on, little one," she said, her voice bright despite the urgency. "We're going on an adventure, just like the heroes in the stories!"

The boy looked up at her, his eyes wide with fear. But Ariadne's infectious smile and the mention of an adventure seemed to spark a glimmer of excitement. He nodded, gripping his toy tightly as Ariadne led him back to his mother.

As they moved forward, Ariadne continued to weave through the crowd, her words of encouragement ringing out like a bell. "Stick together, everyone! We're almost there!" She locked eyes with a group of teenage girls, their faces pale with fear. "Hey, I bet you're all strong swimmers, right? The ships could use some brave helpers like you!"

The girls exchanged glances, their fear slowly giving way to a sense of purpose. They nodded, falling into step behind Ariadne as she forged ahead. As they neared the docks, the scent of salt and tar grew stronger, mingling with the acrid tang of sulfur in the air. The sound of creaking wood and shouting voices filled their ears, a cacophony of urgency and desperation.

Callista paused at the edge of the docks, her eyes scanning the scene before her. Ships of all sizes bobbed in the choppy waters, their decks crowded with frightened Therans clutching meager belongings. Sailors and fishermen worked frantically to load supplies and guide people aboard, their faces glistening with sweat and ash.

For a moment, Callista felt a flicker of doubt. Could they truly evacuate an entire city in the face of such imminent destruction? The task seemed insurmountable, the weight of responsibility crushing.

But as she watched Ariadne guide a group of children to a waiting ship, their small faces alight with tentative hope, Callista felt her resolve strengthen. She drew in a deep breath, the salt air filling her lungs, and squared her shoulders.

They would not fail. They could not. Potnia had shown her the way, and Callista would see her people to safety, no matter the cost.

"Dorian," Captain Minoas called out from the bow of his ship as it approached their dock, "We're here! Tell the High Priestess you four need to get on board quickly! Then help us, we need to distribute the weight more evenly. Too many on one side and we'll capsize before we even leave the harbor."

Dorian nodded, his eyes scanning the deck of the ship as he clambered on board. "You heard the man! Balance the load, and make sure everyone's secure. We've got a long journey ahead of us."

Ariadne darted between the ships, her red hair a vibrant flash amidst the dull grays of ash and smoke. She helped children over the railings, her smile a reassuring constant despite the fear in her own heart.

"There you go, little one," she murmured, settling a small girl onto the deck. "You're safe now. The Great Mother will watch over us all."

As the last stragglers boarded the ships, Callista felt a hand on her shoulder. She turned to see Theron, his face streaked with soot and his eyes filled with worry.

Chapter 17: A Priestess's Plea

"High Priestess," a young woman approached, her voice trembling. "What will become of us? Where will we go?"

Callista took the woman's hands in her own, her gaze warm and reassuring. "The Mother will guide us, child. We must trust in her wisdom and in the strength of our people."

As the woman nodded, comforted by Callista's words, her sight finally followed Theron's and what she saw drew her attention. Lykos emerged on the dock below them, his sycophantic cultists behind him, his eyes wild, and his face contorted with rage.

"You fools!" he bellowed, his voice cutting through the air. "You have doomed us all by following this False Priestess!"

Callista stepped forward to the railing of the ship, her voice calm but firm. "Lykos, your words hold no power here. The people have chosen their path, and we will not be swayed by your fear and doubt any longer!"

Lykos sneered, his hands clenching into fists. "You think you have won, Callista? You are nothing but a puppet of the Mother, a pawn in her game."

Callista shook her head, a hint of sadness in her eyes. "It is you who are the puppet, Lykos. A puppet of your own ambition and pride. But there is still hope for you, if you choose to embrace it."

For a moment, Lykos wavered, his anger faltering in the face of Callista's compassion. But then his eyes hardened once more, and he turned away, disappearing into the shadows of the thickening ash cloud that hung over Akrotiri.

Callista sighed, her heart heavy with the knowledge that some wounds ran too deep to heal. "We are the Children of Potnia," she declared, her voice ringing out across the waves. "And together, we will find our way to a new home."

Lykos's voice cut through the crowded ships and surrounding docks like a knife. "Foolishness!" he bellowed, his eyes blazing with anger. "The High Priestess leads you astray, spinning tales of false hope and abandon!"

Callista turned to face him, her chin held high. She could feel the weight of her people's gaze upon her, the fragile threads of their trust hanging in the balance.

"I lead our people to survival," she said, her voice ringing out clear and true. "I offer them a path forward, guided by the wisdom of Potnia herself."

Lykos sneered, his hands clenching into fists at his sides. "You offer them lies and delusion! You would have them turn their backs on the sacred traditions of Thera!"

But even as he spoke, Callista could see the doubt in the eyes of those who followed him. His words, once so powerful, now rang hollow in the face of the trio's unwavering conviction.

"Enough, Lykos," Theron said, his voice calm but firm. "The people have made their choice. It is time to let go of the past and embrace the future. You who stand with Lykos now, we have room on these ships for you!"

Lykos's face twisted with rage, because he could see the truth in Theron's words. His influence, once so strong, was crumbling like the walls of Akrotiri beneath the mountain's fury.

Callista stepped forward, her voice ringing out over the murmurs of the crowd. "People of Thera, hear me now. The path ahead may be uncertain, but we must not let fear guide our steps. We are the children of Potnia, and She has shown us the way."

She turned to face Lykos, her green eyes blazing with conviction. "You speak of tradition, Lykos, but what good is tradition if it leads us to our doom? The world is changing, and we must change with it if we hope to survive."

Lykos's face reddened with anger, his fists clenching at his sides. "You would have us abandon our sacred duties, our very way of life! This is blasphemy!"

But Callista held her ground, her voice steady and sure. "No, Lykos. This is not blasphemy. This is the will of the Mother Herself. She has sent us signs, warnings of the danger that lurks beneath our feet. And now, She has given us a chance to escape, to start anew in a land beyond this island."

She turned to the ships around her and raised her voice wo all could hear over the tumult, her arms outstretched in a gesture of unity. "We are all Her children, and She loves us all equally. Rich or poor, highborn or low, we all have a place in Her plan. And that plan leads us to safety, to a future where our children and our children's children can thrive."

As she spoke, Callista could feel the energy of her people, of Thera, the fear and uncertainty giving way to a sense of purpose and determination. She saw the light of hope kindling in their eyes, and she knew that her words had struck a chord deep within their hearts.

But Lykos would not relent, nor would he let his cultists board the ships. He turned to them, his voice dripping with venom. "Do not listen to her lies! The High Priestess leads you astray, blinded by false visions of glory. We will stay and honor the traditions of our ancestors, not flee like cowards."

The cultists hesitated, torn between loyalty to Lykos and the stirring words of Callista. Some looked to the ships, their eyes filled with longing for a chance at survival. Others clenched their fists, swayed by Lykos's desperate rhetoric.

Callista stepped closer to the ship's railing, her eyes locking onto his steely gaze. "Lykos, do not let your pride cloud your judgment. The Mother has shown us a path to safety, a chance to preserve our sacred traditions in a new land. Do not let fear and bitterness drive you to ruin. If you wish to die on the island then so be it, but don't take those people with you!"

But Lykos remained unmoved, his jaw set in stubborn defiance. "I will not abandon everything we hold dear for the whims of a so-called prophetess." He turned to the cultists around him. "I AM THE PRIEST-KING OF THERA! I ALONE CAN SAVE OUR HOME! FOLLOW ME NOW TO THE PRECIPICE AND I WILL LEAD US TO A NEW DAWN, A BETTER DAY FOR ALL OF THERA!" Lykos and his sycophants turned and walked into the darkening streets of Akrotiri in the direction of the mountain.

Callista turned from them, tears streaming down her face, making deep ravines in the ash that dirtied her beautiful visage. She looked from Dorian to Theron, Ariadne, and finally on the Captain. "It is time to go." She whispered. Her voice, her soul, spent.

Chapter 18: Wrath of the Earth

Lykos stood defiantly on the mountain path, his eyes blazing with a fervor bordering on madness. The volcanic earth trembled beneath his sandaled feet, a portent of the cataclysm to come. Yet he remained unshaken, his voice booming over the ominous rumble.

"Do you feel it, my devoted followers?" Lykos swept his arms wide, the folds of his ceremonial robes billowing in the sulfurous wind. "Pyragetes speaks to us through the very ground! This fissure is no mere geological oddity - it is a divine gateway, a searing summons from our great god within the mountain!"

The gathered cultists shifted uneasily, their faces a mottled canvas of fear and desperate belief. Many clutched carved totems and amulets, seeking solace in the familiar weight of polished stone against their palms.

Lykos' lips curled in a smile that held no warmth. These lost souls, so hungry for purpose, for meaning in a chaotic world. How easily they could be molded, their doubts smelted into unquestioning loyalty within the crucible of his words.

"Pyragetes demands proof of our devotion!" Lykos' sonorous tones swelled, drowning out the mountain's groans. "And what greater testament of faith could there be than offering ourselves to his embrace? To become one with the living flame at Thera's heart!"

The cultists' murmurs rose in pitch, a discordant choir wavering between reverence and dread. Lykos drank in their conflicted expressions with a raptor's pitiless gaze.

"Cast aside your earthly tethers! Relinquish your attachments to the mundane world and clothe yourselves in courage! Let your spirits soar unfettered into His smoldering depths!"

Lykos thrust a commanding finger toward the seething chasm, his eyes alight with the promise of glory. Thera's fate hung in the balance, teetering on a knife's edge between salvation and annihilation. And he,

Lykos Theodoros, would be the fulcrum upon which it all pivoted - the priest-king who delivered his people unto the very maw of their true god.

He drew himself up to his full height, a conduit of holy purpose. "Who among you possesses the mettle to be first? To blaze a trail of faith into the fiery heart of our Lord?"

The cultists trembled like reeds before a rising gale, their souls locked in a battle between self-preservation and the desire for cosmic significance. Lykos' words had kindled a blaze in their hearts, an inferno that threatened to consume all reason.

As he watched them grapple with their convictions, a thrill of savage satisfaction surged through Lykos' veins. Piece by piece, he was inexorably realizing his grand vision - a world reforged in the name of Pyragetes, where he reigned supreme as the god's anointed emissary. And these obedient acolytes, so eager to martyr themselves, were but the kindling to ignite his glorious ascent.

"Step forward, my chosen ones!" Lykos' voice thundered, echoing off the mountain's flanks. "Pyragetes awaits your sacrifice! Let us prove ourselves worthy of His blessings and deliver Thera from calamity!"

The ground shuddered more violently now, as if the island itself strained to contain the building pressures within. Lykos stood firm at the precipice, a messiah poised to lead his flock into the scorching maw of their volcanic god - and perhaps, to their ultimate doom. Lykos extended his arm, pointing to the gaping fissure before them. The heat from the molten lava below wafted upwards, distorting the air with a shimmering haze. Beads of sweat formed on the brows of the cultists, their faces illuminated by the hellish glow emanating from the depths.

They exchanged nervous glances, their loyalty to Lykos warring with the primal instinct for survival. The weight of their faith pressed down upon them, urging them to take that fateful step, to surrender themselves to the fiery embrace of their god.

One man, his robes billowing in the scorching updraft, stepped forward. His eyes were wide with a mixture of terror and exaltation, his breath coming in ragged gasps. He hesitated at the edge, his toes curling over the brink as he peered into the seething abyss below. Lykos watched him intently, his own heart pounding with anticipation. This was the moment of truth, the ultimate test of devotion. Would the cultist falter, or would he leap into the arms of Pyragetes, setting an example for the others to follow?

The man's resolve wavered, his body trembling as he confronted the magnitude of the sacrifice demanded of him. Lykos could see the doubt etched in the lines of his face, the flicker of self-preservation struggling against the tide of blind faith.

"Brother," Lykos called out, his voice a beacon of encouragement amidst the roar of the mountain. "Pyragetes awaits your brave soul. Let your faith be your wings, and soar into His divine embrace!"

The cultist drew a shuddering breath, his eyes locking with Lykos' for a fleeting moment. In that shared gaze, a silent understanding passed between them - a recognition of the power of belief, and the lengths to which it could drive a mortal soul.

Then, with a final cry that was equal parts terror and exultation, the man leaped forward, his body plummeting into the incandescent depths of the fissure. The other cultists gasped, some averting their eyes while others watched in morbid fascination as their comrade vanished into the molten heart of the mountain.

Lykos felt a surge of triumph, his lips curving into a smile that was at once beatific and terrifying. The first sacrifice had been made, a powerful statement of faith that would surely inspire the others to follow suit. He turned to face his remaining acolytes, his eyes blazing with the fervor of a man who believed himself to be the instrument of divine will.

"Who among you will be next?" he asked, his voice ringing out like a clarion call. "Who will join our brave brother in the crucible of Pyragetes' love, and emerge reborn as a true champion of the faith?"

The ground shook once more, the mountain's rumble rising to a deafening crescendo. Lykos stood tall amidst the chaos, a prophet on the brink of apocalypse, ready to guide his flock into the searing embrace of their god - no matter the cost.

One by one, the cultists stepped forward, their faces a mix of fear and rapture. They had come this far, driven by Lykos' unshakable conviction and their own desperate need to believe in something greater than themselves. Now, with the first sacrifice made, there was no turning back.

A woman, her dark hair whipping in the scorching wind, approached the edge of the fissure. She paused for a moment, her eyes meeting Lykos' in a silent plea for guidance. He nodded, his expression a mask of solemn encouragement, and she took a deep breath before leaping into the abyss, her scream echoing off the rocky walls as she disappeared from view.

Another followed, and then another, each one driven by a potent cocktail of terror and exhilaration. Some wept openly as they jumped, their tears evaporating in the searing heat of the lava below. Others laughed, a mad, desperate sound that spoke of a mind pushed beyond the brink of reason.

Lykos watched, his heart swelling with a dark pride. These were his people, his chosen ones, and they were willing to give their very lives for the cause. With each sacrifice, he felt his power grow, the mountain's fury becoming an extension of his own indomitable will.

The air grew thick with the stench of burning flesh and sulfur, a choking miasma that seared the lungs and stung the eyes. Still, the cultists came, driven by the implacable force of Lykos' charisma and their own unshakable faith. They leaped into the fissure with abandon, their cries of devotion and terror mingling in a cacophonous chorus that rose to the heavens.

And through it all, the mountain roared, the ground shaking beneath their feet as if in anticipation of the cataclysm to come. Lykos stood at the center of the maelstrom, a prophet and a madman, ready to lead his flock into the very heart of oblivion.

As the last cultist teetered on the edge of the fissure, the ground beneath Lykos' feet heaved violently, nearly throwing him off balance. The air thrummed with a deep, primal energy, as if the very heart of the earth was about to burst forth from its rocky confines.

Lykos threw his arms wide, his eyes blazing with a feverish light. "Behold!" he cried, his voice rising above the deafening rumble. "The power of Pyragetes is upon us! Our sacrifices have pleased him, and now he will spare our island from destruction!"

The cultist hesitated, glancing back at Lykos with a mixture of awe and terror. Lykos met his gaze, his own eyes filled with an unshakable conviction. "Jump," he commanded, his voice barely audible above the roar of the mountain. "Join your brothers and sisters in the eternal embrace of the sacred fires of Pyragetes."

For a moment, the cultist wavered, caught between the primal urge to flee and the overwhelming power of Lykos' will. Then, with a final, desperate cry, he leaped into the abyss, his body consumed by the hungry flames below.

Lykos raised his arms to the sky, his voice rising in a triumphant shout. "Pyragetes, hear me!" he cried, his words carried aloft on the scorching wind. "We have proven our devotion! Now, spare your faithful servants and grant us your divine protection!"

But even as the words left his lips, the earth beneath his feet split open with a deafening crack. A massive plume of ash and fire erupted from the depths of the mountain, consuming everything in its path. The searing heat blasted Lykos backward, the force of the explosion sending him tumbling head over heels.

For a moment, he lay stunned, his ears ringing and his vision blurred. Then, as the realization of what had happened sank in, his triumphant expression slowly transformed into one of utter shock and disbelief.

It... it cannot be, he thought, his mind reeling. I did everything right. I offered the sacrifices, I led my people with unwavering faith. How could Pyragetes abandon us now?

But as the ground shook and the fire roared, Lykos knew that his hubris had finally caught up with him. He had dared to challenge the gods themselves, and now he would pay the ultimate price for his arrogance.

***

The ship rocked violently as the shockwaves from the eruption rippled across the sea. Callista gripped the railing tightly, her knuckles white with the effort. Beside her, Dorian and Theron struggled to maintain their footing on the heaving deck.

"By the gods," Theron whispered, his voice barely audible above the roar of the waves. "I've never seen anything like it."

Callista nodded, her eyes fixed on where her island had been. Flames danced along the coastline, casting an eerie orange glow against the darkening sky. A massive column of ash and smoke billowed upwards to impossible heights, obscuring the once-familiar landscape.

"It's all gone," she said softly, her voice thick with emotion. "Everything we've ever known, everything we've ever loved. It's all gone."

Dorian moved closer, his arm sliding around her shoulders in a gesture of comfort. "We did everything we could," he said gently. "You saved so many lives, Callista. Don't ever forget that."

She leaned into his embrace, drawing strength from his presence. "But what about those we couldn't save?" she asked, her gaze still locked on the burning island. "What about all the people who refused to leave, who believed in Lykos and his twisted faith?"

Theron shook his head, his expression somber and embraced both Callista and Dorian. "They made their choice," he said quietly. "We can only hope that they find peace in the afterlife."

Callista closed her eyes, a single tear sliding down her cheek. She thought of her family, her friends, all the people she had known and loved throughout her life on Thera. Were they safe? Had they managed to escape the destruction, or had they perished in the flames?

“Potnia, Great Mother,” she prayed quietly, watch over your children in this dark hour. “Guide us through the storm and lead us to safety.”

As if in answer to her prayer, the ship suddenly lurched forward, propelled by a powerful gust of wind. The sails billowed outwards, straining against the rigging as the vessel surged through the choppy waters.

"Look!" Dorian exclaimed, pointing towards the horizon. "The wind is changing. It's blowing us away from the island."

Callista opened her eyes, hope flaring in her heart. Perhaps the gods had heard her prayer after all. Perhaps they were not entirely forsaken.

She turned to Dorian and Theron, a newfound determination etched on her face. "We may have lost our home," she said, her voice growing stronger with each word, "but we still have each other. We still have a future. And we will build a new life, a better life, no matter where the winds may take us."

Theron's knuckles whitened as he gripped the railing, his analytical mind racing to comprehend the scale of the destruction that had unfolded before them. The once-peaceful island, now a seething cauldron of fire and ash, seemed to have torn itself apart from within. His heart ached for the lives lost, for the centuries of history and knowledge consumed by the relentless flames.

As the trio stood united, their shared sorrow and determination binding them together, Theron's keen eyes spotted a new threat emerging from the chaos. A massive wave, born from the violent upheaval of the island, raced towards their ship, its foaming crest towering above the surrounding swells.

"Brace yourselves!" Theron shouted, his voice cutting through the air like a knife. "A great wave approaches!"

Dorian sprang into action, his years of seafaring experience guiding his movements as he barked orders to the crew. "Captain! Secure the rigging! secure the hatches to the hold! We must prepare to ride out the wave!"

The Captain echoed Dorian's warning, making it a command to his crew. The deck became a flurry of activity as sailors rushed to follow Dthe commands, their faces grim with determination. Callista, her robes whipping about her in the rising wind, closed her eyes and began to pray, her lips moving in a silent invocation to the gods.

Theron, his mind racing with calculations and possibilities, turned to his companions, a flicker of hope sparking in his eyes. "If we can angle the ship just right, we might be able to use the wave's momentum to carry us to safety."

Dorian grinned, a flash of his characteristic optimism breaking through the tension. "Leave it to you, my friend, to find a way to turn even the greatest of challenges into a chance for survival."

Chapter 19: Gone With the Tides

Dorian gripped the wheel of the ship, his knuckles white as the towering wave bore down on the ship. He had rushed to take over the helm at the Captain's urging. "Brace yourselves!" he shouted above the roar of the sea. "Reef the mainsail! Grab hold of anything you can!"

The crew and the civilians scrambled to obey, their voices rising in a cacophony of shouts and prayers. Dorian's heart pounded in his chest, but he kept his voice steady.

Beside him, Theron clutched the railing, his eyes narrowed against the salt spray. "Steer her into the wave!" the Captain called out from the bow of the ship. "Thirty degrees to port! We'll take the brunt of it head-on."

Dorian nodded grimly. He spun the wheel, feeling the deck pitch beneath his feet as the ship turned to face the oncoming swell.

"Potnia, Mother of the Seas, guide us through," Dorian murmured under his breath. He pictured the goddess as the priestesses depicted her, draped in foam-white robes with a crown of abalone shells. Surely she would not abandon her faithful now.

The wave loomed ahead of them, a mountain of churning water. Dorian braced his legs against the wheel box, his muscles straining as he fought to keep the ship steady. Beside him, Theron began to chant, his voice low and rhythmic. The ancient words of the priesthood rose above the wind, a plea to the Great Mother for deliverance.

For a breathless moment, time seemed to slow. Dorian felt the spray on his face, tasted the salt on his lips. Then the wave crashed over them, and the world dissolved into chaos.

Amidst the chaos, Callista emerged from below deck, her dark hair whipping in the wind. With measured steps, she made her way to the huddled group of refugees stuck up on deck, their faces pale with fear. Kneeling beside them, she took their hands in hers, her voice low and soothing.

"Take heart, children of Potnia," she murmured. "The Mother is with us, even in the heart of the storm. Trust in her, and in the strength of those who guide us."

As she spoke, a sense of calm seemed to settle over the refugees. They clung to her words like a lifeline, their eyes fixed on her serene face. Callista's presence was a balm, her spiritual authority a beacon in the darkness.

Around them, the ship groaned and shuddered, the timbers creaking under the strain. The sails snapped in the wind, the sound sharp and percussive against the roar of the waves. Salt spray hung heavy in the air, coating everything in a slick sheen.

Yet even amid the chaos, the crew worked as one, their movements precise and purposeful. They hauled on lines and adjusted sails, their faces set with grim determination. Their trust in Dorian and the Minoas was absolute, a bond forged among sailors over centuries in the crucible of countless storms.

Callista watched them work, her heart swelling with pride. These were her people, the children of Thera, and they would not be broken by the fury of the sea. She closed her eyes, offering a silent prayer to Potnia.

"Great Mother, guide us through this trial," she whispered. "Let your strength flow through us, and bring us safe to shore."

A shaft of sunlight pierced the clouds as if in answer, gilding the waves with a fleeting brilliance. Callista smiled, her faith unshakable. They would weather this storm, as they had so many others, with the blessing of the Mother and the courage of their hearts.

The wave struck with the force of a titan's fist. The ship tried careening sideways. Dorian's hands tightened on the wheel, his knuckles white with strain as he fought to keep the vessel on course. The deck pitched and rolled beneath his feet, but he held his ground, his eyes fixed on the churning seas ahead.

"Steady on!" he shouted, his voice barely audible above the howling wind.

"We'll ride this out! Just hold fast!" Captain Minoas bellowed.

Beside him, Theron braced himself against the railing, his robes whipping about his legs. He scanned the deck, his keen eyes taking in every detail. A coil of rope had come loose, threatening to tangle in the rigging. He lunged for it, his fingers closing around the rough fibers just as the ship heaved again.

"Secure that line!" he called to a nearby sailor. "And check the cargo! We can't afford to lose any supplies!"

The sailor nodded, his face grim as he set about his task. Theron turned back to Dorian, his voice low and urgent.

"We need to get the refugees below decks," he said. "They'll be safer there."

Dorian nodded, his jaw clenched. "Aye, but we can't risk leaving the wheel. Can you see to it?"

Theron clapped a hand on his friend's shoulder, a gesture of reassurance. "Consider it done."

He made his way across the heaving deck, his steps sure and steady despite the rolling waves. The refugees huddled together with Callista, their faces pale with fear. Theron raised his voice, his tone calm and authoritative.

"Follow me," he said. "We'll get you settled below. You'll be safe there." He looked at Callista, love and fear mingled on the features of his face. “You too Callista.”

She shook her head, “No, I will stay here and give what aid I can to the crew.”

The refugees hesitated, their eyes wide with uncertainty. But Theron's calm demeanor was a source of strength, and slowly, they began to move, following him towards the hatch that led to the lower decks.

As they descended into the darkness, Theron felt a flicker of worry. The ship was strong, but the sea's fury could break even the mightiest vessel. He pushed the thought aside, focusing instead on the task at hand.

"Find a spot and hold on tight," he told the refugees. "We'll come for you when it's safe."

As the ship crested another towering wave, Dorian's heart soared at the sight just over the crest. Calm seas! Then he looked around, and his heart sank at the sight that greeted him. Scattered across the turbulent sea, the other vessels in their fleet struggled against the relentless onslaught of wind and water. Some listed dangerously to the side, their sails tattered and flapping uselessly in the gale. Others had been driven off course, their crews fighting desperately to keep them from capsizing. Others were gone beneath the waves, some smashed to pieces by them. Men, women, and children floundered in the water...

Beside him, Callista and Captain Minoas stood in silent grief, their faces etched with sorrow as they witnessed the devastation. In that moment, the trio shared a profound understanding of life's fragility and the sea's capricious nature. They knew, with a heavy certainty, that not every ship would make it through the storm.

As the immediate danger began to pass, the ship's rolling became less violent, the wind's howling less deafening. Dorian let out a shaky breath, his shoulders sagging with exhaustion and relief. Around him, the crew sprang into action, assessing the damage and beginning the arduous process of repairs.

Theron moved up on deck and to Dorian's side, his hand coming to rest on his shoulder in a gesture of support. "We made it through," he said, his voice hoarse from shouting over the wind.

Dorian nodded, his jaw tight with the effort of holding back his emotions. "We did," he agreed.

"But there's still work to be done. We need to make sure the ship is seaworthy." Said Minoas.

Together, the three men began to make their way around the deck, inspecting the masts and rigging for any signs of damage. The crew worked around them, their faces grim with determination as they patched up torn sails and secured loose cargo.

Amidst the chaos of the storm's aftermath, Callista moved through the ship with a sense of purpose, her green eyes scanning the faces of the injured and frightened. She paused beside a young woman who was clutching her arm, her face contorted in pain.

"Let me see," Callista said gently, kneeling beside the woman and carefully examining the injury. "It's not broken, but it will need to be wrapped."

With deft fingers, Callista tore a strip of cloth from her own robe and began to bind the woman's arm, her touch gentle and reassuring. As she worked, she murmured a quiet prayer, her words seeming to ease the woman's pain and fear.

Around her, the refugees huddled together, their faces etched with exhaustion and grief. Callista moved among them, offering words of comfort and healing, her presence a balm to their battered spirits. She could see Ariadne further down the hold of the ship, doing the same.

"Have faith," she told them, her voice soft but filled with conviction. "The gods have not abandoned us. We will find our way through this darkness."

As the hours passed, Callista tended to the wounded and the weary, her hands never idle. She applied salves to cuts and bruises, whispered prayers over the sick and dying, and offered words of encouragement to those who had lost hope.

Night fell, and the ship sailed on beneath a canopy of stars, the gentle rocking of the waves a soothing contrast to the violence of the storm. On the deck, the crew settled into a weary but hopeful calm, their faces turned towards the heavens in silent gratitude for their survival.

Callista stood at the railing, her dark hair billowing in the cool night breeze. She closed her eyes, breathing in the salty air and letting the peace of the moment wash over her.

Dorian and Theron joined her, their presence a comforting reminder of the bond they shared. In the stillness of the night, they stood together, their hearts heavy with the weight of all they had endured, but filled with a quiet determination to face whatever challenges lay ahead.

"We will find a way," Callista said softly, her eyes fixed on the distant horizon. "The gods have brought us this far. They will not abandon us now."

Dorian and Theron nodded, their own faith bolstered by Callista's unwavering conviction. Together, they gazed up at the stars, the vastness of the sky a reminder of the smallness of their troubles in the grand scheme of things.

As the trio stood in comfortable silence, the gentle rocking of the ship lulled them into a sense of tranquility. Dorian's hand found Callista's, their fingers intertwining as if it were the most natural thing in the world. Theron, standing on Callista's other side, placed a reassuring hand on her shoulder, a silent gesture of support and unity.

"I don't know what I would have done without you both," Callista whispered, her voice barely audible above the distant sound of the waves. "Your strength, your faith... it's what kept me going."

Dorian smiled, his eyes crinkling at the corners. "We're in this together, Callista. No matter what comes our way, we'll face it as one."

Theron nodded in agreement, his voice filled with conviction. "The gods have brought us together for a reason. Our paths are intertwined, our destinies linked."

Callista felt a warmth spread through her chest, a sense of belonging and purpose that she had never experienced before. In the midst of the chaos and uncertainty, she had found something precious: a connection that transcended the boundaries of their individual lives.

As they stood there, the stars above seemed to shimmer with a new intensity, as if the heavens themselves were bearing witness to the bond that had been forged between them. The cool night air carried with it the promise of a new beginning, a chance to rebuild and start anew.

Callista leaned into Theron's embrace, her head resting on his shoulder as Dorian's arm moved to encircle her waist. In that moment, the world around them seemed to fade away, leaving only the three of them, bound together by an unspoken love that defied explanation.

Dorian's voice, soft and tender, broke the silence. "I never thought I could feel this way about anyone, let alone two people. But here, with you both, it feels like I've found a piece of myself I never knew was missing."

Theron's grip tightened. "I've spent my life seeking purpose, searching for a reason behind the trials the gods have sent my way. And now, I realize... it was all leading me to you."

Callista felt tears prick at the corners of her eyes, overwhelmed by the depth of emotion that flowed between them. "I never believed in fate, in the idea that our lives were predetermined by some cosmic force. But this... this feels like destiny."

She turned to face them, her hands reaching out to cup their faces. "I love you both, with every fiber of my being. And no matter what the future holds, I know that our love will be our strength, our guiding light."

Dorian leaned in, his forehead touching hers, as Theron's lips brushed against her temple. In that moment, their hearts beat as one, their souls intertwined in a dance of devotion and desire.

And as they held each other, the stars above seemed to shine a little brighter, as if the very universe was celebrating the love that had blossomed amidst the chaos. For in that brief, perfect moment, nothing else mattered but the connection they shared, the unbreakable bond that would carry them through whatever storms lay ahead.

Chapter 20: Dawn of a New Age

The weathered wooden planks of the ship creaked beneath Callista's sandaled feet as she made her way down the gangplank, Dorian and Theron close behind. Her robes fluttered in the salty breeze, the fabric heavy with the scent of ash from their hasty departure. As her toes sank into the warm, unfamiliar sand, a wave of emotions crashed over her—relief at their survival, grief for all they had lost, and uncertainty about what lay ahead in this new land. An island Dorian said was called Tholos.

Turning back, Callista watched as the other survivors disembarked, their faces etched with weariness and sorrow. Mothers clutched wide-eyed children, elders leaned on makeshift walking sticks, and the able-bodied carried what meager supplies they had salvaged. They gathered around her on the beach, desperate for guidance and reassurance.

Taking a deep breath, Callista raised her voice to address the huddled crowd. "People of Thera, my brothers and sisters, I know your hearts are heavy with grief and your bodies weary from the journey. But I ask you now to lift your eyes and behold the land the Great Mother has delivered us to." She gestured to the lush green hills rising beyond the sand.

"Though we have lost much, we still have each other, and together we will build a new home here, guided by the wisdom of Potnia." Her words hung in the salt-tinged air for a moment before Dorian stepped forward, his hand coming to rest on her shoulder.

"Well said, Callista," he murmured, his warm brown eyes meeting hers. "This is a beginning, not an end. We're alive and we have a chance to start over, to create something new and beautiful here on Tholos."

Theron nodded, his gaze already roaming the landscape, no doubt cataloging every plant and rock formation. "Potnia has blessed us with fertile ground and fresh water. We have all the elements needed to thrive, if we work together."

A murmur rippled through the crowd, the first tentative smiles appearing on tear-streaked faces. Children wiggled free from their mothers' grasps, eager to explore the beach. A lightness seemed to settle over the survivors, the first glimmer of hope since the catastrophe that had driven them from their homes.

Callista felt it too, blooming in her chest like a fragile flower. Perhaps the Great Mother had a plan for them after all, a new destiny waiting to unfold on these unfamiliar shores. With Dorian and Theron by her side, and the resilience of her people to sustain them, anything was possible. "We will begin anew here, in this natural, sheltered harbor. Let our new port be called Gera, in honor of Potnia's son." The survivors of Thera looked delighted as many nodded in approval and spoke among themselves excitedly.

Dorian moved among the survivors, his voice carrying over the din of activity as he helped organize the unloading of supplies. "The tents should go there, near the treeline for shelter from the wind. And let's create a central area for cooking and gathering, close to the freshwater stream."

People hurried to follow his instructions, a sense of purpose replacing the earlier despair. Theron joined him, his keen eyes assessing their surroundings. "We should send out scouting parties to survey the area more thoroughly. Look for edible plants, medicinal herbs, and any signs of wildlife."

Dorian nodded, his gaze sweeping over the bustling camp. "Good thinking. We'll need to understand our new environment if we're going to make a home here."

As the two men coordinated their efforts, Callista watched with a mix of pride and gratitude. They were a well-matched team, Dorian's natural leadership and charisma balanced by Theron's quiet intellect and attention to detail. She couldn't imagine facing this challenge without them by her side.

Theron beckoned her over, his expression thoughtful. "Callista, come see this." He led her to the edge of the treeline, where a rocky outcropping overlooked a lush valley. "The soil here is rich and dark, perfect for farming. And did you notice our harbor? It's dark waters are more than deep enough for ships to dock, which will open up trade and fishing opportunities."

Callista followed his gaze, her heart quickening at the possibilities. "You're right. This land has everything we need to build a new life." She turned to Dorian, who had joined them on the ridge.

As the sun began to dip towards the horizon, Callista gathered the survivors around a large, flat stone that would serve as an altar. She draped a simple white cloth over the stone and placed a small figurine of Potnia at its center, surrounded by a wreath of wildflowers they had gathered from the nearby meadow.

Callista raised her hands, and a hush fell over the crowd. "People of Thera," she began, her voice clear and strong, "we have endured much to reach this new land. Our journey has been one of sorrow and loss, but also of hope and resilience. Today, as we begin to build our new home, let us call upon the blessings of our beloved goddess Potnia."

The survivors bowed their heads as Callista began to pray, her words rising and falling like the rhythm of the waves against the shore. "Great Potnia, Mother of All, we ask for your guidance and protection as we establish our new settlement of Gera, named after your blessed son. Bless this land with fertility and abundance, and grant us the strength and wisdom to create a community that honors your sacred ways."

As Callista spoke, Theron and Dorian moved among the crowd, lighting small clay lamps that each person held. The flickering light cast a warm glow over the gathering, a symbol of the hope and unity that bound them together.

"May our lives here be a testament to your grace, and may we never forget the lessons of our past as we build towards a brighter future," Callista concluded, her eyes shining with emotion. "In your name, we pray. Potnia, watch over us. Gera, bless us!"

"Potnia, watch over us, Gera bless us!" the crowd echoed, their voices rising into the twilight air.

As the ceremony concluded, a sense of purpose and determination settled over the survivors. They knew that the work ahead would be challenging, but they were ready to face it head-on.

Callista, Dorian, and Theron led by example, rolling up their sleeves and diving into the tasks at hand. They helped to unload the remaining supplies from the ships, carried water from the nearby stream, and worked alongside the others to clear the land for the first shelters.

Despite the hardships they had faced, laughter and song soon filled the air as the survivors worked together. They shared stories of their old lives in Thera, reminisced about loved ones lost, and dreamed aloud about the future they would build together.

As the first stars began to appear in the darkening sky, Callista paused to catch her breath, leaning against a tree at the edge of the clearing. She watched as her people worked together, their faces illuminated by the warm glow of the torches and lamps.

As the sun dipped below the horizon, the community gathered around a large bonfire, the flickering flames casting a warm glow on their faces. The aroma of roasting meat and herbs filled the air, making stomachs growl in anticipation. Laughter and chatter mingled with the crackling of the fire, creating a symphony of joy and relief.

Callista, Dorian, and Theron sat together on a large log, their shoulders touching as they surveyed the scene before them. Callista's eyes shone with pride as she watched her people, their resilience and spirit unbroken despite the trials they had endured.

"We've come so far," she murmured, her voice barely audible above the din of the celebration. "But there's still so much to do."

Dorian nodded, his hand finding hers in the darkness. "True, but we'll face it together. Our people are strong, and with the blessings of Potnia, we'll build a new home that honors your past while embracing our future."

Theron leaned forward, his elbows resting on his knees. "Speaking of our future, we should discuss our plans for the settlement. We need to strike a balance between preserving our traditions and adapting to this new land."

Callista turned to him, her brow furrowed in thought. "You're right. We can't simply recreate Thera here, but we also can't abandon our way of life entirely. Perhaps we can start by identifying the most essential elements of our culture and finding ways to integrate them into our new reality."

Dorian chuckled, his eyes twinkling in the firelight. "Like the importance of a good feast!" He gestured to the celebration around them. "But in all seriousness, I believe our trading skills and maritime knowledge will serve us well here. We can establish new trade routes and alliances with the neighboring settlements."

Theron nodded, his gaze distant as he considered the possibilities. "And we mustn't forget the importance of agriculture. This land is fertile, and with careful planning, we can ensure a sustainable food supply for our people."

The conversation flowed easily between the three leaders, each offering insights and ideas born from their unique experiences and expertise. They discussed the layout of the settlement, the allocation of resources, and the roles and responsibilities of the community members.

As the night wore on and the celebration began to wind down, Callista felt a sense of peace settle over her. The path ahead was still uncertain, but with Dorian and Theron by her side, and the support of her people, she knew they would find their way.

She stood, her voice ringing out clear and strong. "My friends, my family, tonight we celebrate our survival and the promise of a new beginning. Tomorrow, we begin the work of building our future. It won't be easy, but together, we will create a home that will stand the test of time. A home that will honor the memory of Thera and the blessings of Potnia. A home that will be a beacon of hope and strength for generations to come."

The people cheered, their voices rising into the night sky like a prayer. And as the last embers of the bonfire faded into darkness, Callista, Dorian, and Theron stood hand in hand, ready to face whatever challenges lay ahead, together.

As the first light of dawn painted the sky in hues of pink and gold on their 23rd day on Tholos building their new capital Gera, Callista stood before the assembled community, her heart thrumming with nervous anticipation. Beside her, Dorian and Theron radiated a calm resolve, their presence a steadying force in the face of the momentous occasion.

The trio had spent the early hours of the morning in quiet preparation, each lost in their own thoughts and prayers. Now, as they faced their people, Callista felt a surge of love and gratitude for the two men who had become her anchors in the storm.

She took a deep breath, her voice carrying across the gathered crowd. "People of Tholos, of Gera! Today marks a new chapter in our story. A chapter of unity, of strength, and of hope. Today, we come before you not just as leaders, but as partners in every sense of the word."

Dorian stepped forward, his hand finding Callista's. "In the face of adversity, we have found solace and support in one another. Our bond has been forged in the crucible of shared hardship and shared purpose. And now, we wish to formalize that bond before the eyes of our community and the blessing of Potnia herself."

Theron joined them, his voice steady and sure. "We stand before you today to exchange vows of commitment, not just to each other, but to our people. To lead with compassion, with wisdom, and with unwavering dedication to the wellbeing of Gera and all who call it home."

“We are the Triad spoken of in the ancient scrolls of our people, it is our blessed burden to continue to lead you as three people forming a single bond, now that we’ve led you here to a new beginning!” Callista declared.

A murmur rippled through the crowd, surprise mingling with curiosity and a growing sense of acceptance. Callista felt her heart swell with emotion as she turned to face Dorian and Theron, their hands clasped in hers.

In turn, they spoke their vows, their words weaving a tapestry of love, loyalty, and shared purpose. They pledged their hearts to one another and their lives to the service of their people, their voices ringing out clear and strong in the morning air. As the final words of the ceremony faded away, Callista felt a sense of rightness settle over her. This was the path they were meant to walk, side by side, hand in hand.

She turned to face the community again, her voice filled with conviction. "People of Gera, we stand before you today as your leaders, your protectors, and your servants. We pledge to guide you with wisdom, to defend you with courage, and to work tirelessly for the betterment of our new home."

Dorian spoke next, his words painting a picture of the future they envisioned. "Together, we will build a society that honors the traditions of your past while embracing the possibilities of our future. We will foster innovation and creativity, while remaining rooted in the values that have sustained us through the darkest of times."

Theron's voice rang out, strong and clear. "We will face challenges, as all communities do. But we will face them together, united in our determination to create a legacy of resilience and hope. We will learn from one another, support one another, and grow together as we navigate this new path."

As the trio's words washed over the assembled crowd, Callista saw a flicker of hope in the eyes of her people. A sense of purpose, of belonging, of shared destiny.

And as the sun rose over the horizon, bathing the gathering in golden light, Callista knew that whatever trials lay ahead, they would face them as one. A community bound by love, by faith, and by the unbreakable ties of family.

A gentle murmur rippled through the crowd as the trio concluded their address. Callista's eyes scanned the faces of her people, trying to gauge their reactions. Some, like old Nestor the fisherman, wore expressions of uncertainty, their brows furrowed as they processed the implications of this new leadership. Others, like young Iantha, the weaver's daughter, couldn't contain their excitement, their eyes sparkling with the promise of a brighter future.

Callista's heart swelled as she watched Dorian and Theron move among the crowd, their easy smiles and warm words helping to ease any lingering doubts. She overheard snippets of conversation, the tone gradually shifting from cautious to hopeful.

"I never thought I'd see the day when a priestess would marry not one, but two men," chuckled Dion, the potter. "But if anyone can make it work, it's those three."

"I always knew there was something special about Callista," added his wife, Daphne. "And Dorian and Theron, they're good men. They'll lead us well."

As the community began to disperse, heading off to continue the work of building their new home, Callista felt a gentle hand on her shoulder. She turned to see Eirene, her mentor and friend, her eyes brimming with emotion.

"I am so proud of you, my dear," Eirene whispered, pulling Callista into a warm embrace. "You have grown into a leader of great wisdom and compassion. Potnia has truly blessed us all."

Callista returned the hug, feeling tears prick at the corners of her eyes. "Thank you, Eirene. Your guidance has meant everything to me. I only hope I can live up to the faith you all have placed in us."

As the two women parted, Callista caught sight of Dorian and Theron, their faces alight with joy as they spoke with members of the community. Her heart swelled with love for these two remarkable men, and for the people they had all sworn to serve.

"We will build a future worthy of our past," she murmured, a silent prayer to Potnia and her son Gera. "A future of hope, of unity, and of love."

And with that, Callista stepped forward to join her husbands, ready to face whatever challenges lay ahead, secure in the knowledge that they would face them together.

Don't miss out!

Visit the website below and you can sign up to receive emails whenever Sarah Princeps publishes a new book. There's no charge and no obligation.

https://books2read.com/r/B-A-FQEID-ICUBG

BOOKS 2 READ

Connecting independent readers to independent writers.